INTO the FOREST

S.R. JAYE

S.R. Jaye

http://www.SRJaye.com

Publisher's Note: This is a work of fiction. Names, characters, places, and incidents are a product of the author's imagination. Locales and public names are sometimes used for atmospheric purposes. Any resemblance to actual people, living or dead, or to businesses, companies, events, institutions, or locales is completely coincidental.

Cover Design: J. Robinson Designs

Illustrations: Larka Studio

Maps: J. Robinson Designs, watercolored by Larka Studio

Into the Forest/S.R. Jaye. — 1st ed.

Name Pronunciation Guide

Amberflayer—**AM**-ber-flay-er

Andilet—**AN**-di-lay

Arjun—**AR**-jun

Aurantius—ah-**RON**-chee-us

Brassica—**BRASS**-sick-ah

Brickasius—bri-**KAY**-shus

Brinley—**BRIN**-lee

Calibrae—cah-**LEE**-bray

Carnelion—car-**NEE**-lee-un

Cashcoch—**CASH**-cock

Catri—**CAT**-tree

Cinnabar—**SIN**-a-bar

Cretillon—**KREH**-til-on

Dandolian—dan-**DOH**-lee-un

Drugarda—drew-**GAR**-duh

Elodie—**EL**-oh-dee

Ermias—er-**MY**-us

Fanger—**FANG**-ur

Goldaris—goal-**DARE**-us
Isatis—eye-**SAY**-tis
Jezellion—juh-**ZEL**-yun
Kylan—**KYE**-lun
Landyn—**LAN**-din
LuxLuman—**LUX**-**LOO**-mun
Maisie—**MAY**-zee
Maurelle—more-**ELL**
Porfirio—poor-**FEAR**-ee-oh
Raiden—**RAY**-dun
Ronia—**RON**-ya
Rubescent—rue-**BESS**-ent
Rylan—**RYE**-lun
Salamandrini—**SAL**-uh-man-**DREE**-nee
Sinopia—sin-**OH**-pee-ah
Vahlronia—val-**RAHN**-ee-uh
Vermillion—ver-**MILL**-ee-un

CHAPTER I
BLUE MOON

M aisie

The Doove

The last of the twilight was rapidly fading. Soon I'd be operating almost blind. No human eye could adjust to the ominous all-enveloping black dark of the Doove Dorca, especially at night. I pulled my cloak tighter, but mere cloth couldn't warm away the fearful chill so strong that it reached for my soul. Never had I prayed so hard that a witch would be right about the weather. Or hoped so emphatically that the promised blue moonlight would cut through the oppressing gloom of this foreboding forest. That it would reach its tangled floor.

It was full autumn in the human realm—a season I loved, steeped with brilliant warm color and beauty both melancholy and full of hope. If the state of the vegetation around me was any real indication of season, it was autumn here, too, deep in the borderland between the home of the fae and those of us who were merely mortal.

The season didn't bode well for finding the rose the witch Maurelle had sworn I needed if she were to help me. Had promised would bloom in the light of tonight's blue moon. Outside the forest, the frosts had already been worryingly heavy. Blooms were long gone, and bushes were heavy with red and orange rosehips. Trusting a witch in any matter went against my nature and plain common sense. Now it seemed that her knowledge of vegetation was suspect, too. But what choice did I have?

As I picked my way through the overgrown underbrush, a twig snapped beneath my foot. I jumped and nearly dropped the pink-handled dagger I carried, not so much for protection, but for pruning. I froze, heart pounding, watching the shadows that seemed to be watching me. Listening for the sounds of being followed in the gentle rustling of the trees and the call of the night owl.

Maurelle had warned me to leave any lanterns behind. Too much temptation. "Not so much as a pinprick of light. The slightest sparkle will alert the fae and the creatures who dwell in the forest to your presence."

Then she'd armed me with directions to the glen where the rose supposedly grew and a balm that was supposed to mask my human scent. "Bring a sharp knife. The rosebush won't easily give up its flower. I need the rose and its stem intact—a long stem. Cut it as soon as it blooms, while the light of the full moon shines directly on it and you can still see well enough to do the job.

"You'll have just minutes to act before the forest rejects the light and shrouds the rose in darkness. If you hesitate, or are an instant too late, you'll be at the forest's mercy. Lost forever. No one will be able to help you, not even me.

"Once you have the rose, it will guide you out of the forest and home. The fae and forest monsters fear the power of its light. As long as the rose is in your possession, nothing in the forest can harm you."

Reassuring. If Maurelle was telling the truth.

I still didn't trust the shadows, but hearing nothing but the murmur of the forest, I pressed on.

I had lived nearly my entire life just outside the boundaries of this strange forest, watching its seasons from the relative safety of the mortal world. But I had never dared venture in even one small step, let alone deep enough to guess at what kind of plants lay within.

The fringes of the forest that we could see from our cottage window were dense with underbrush so thick no light penetrated more than a few feet in. Even the animals seemed to avoid the Doove. Rabbit and deer skirted it, afraid of the predators that lived in the deep dark. In bad winters, I'd seen deer so thin and starving that their ribs showed, and still they weren't tempted by the lush vegetation of the forest. Along with the fae, the Doove was full of mythically fast and ravenous wolves and cougar, things that could make a quick meal of small prey and small girls. My dagger was surely meager protection against them.

Our whole lives, as long as she lived, Mother had kept a close eye on both Catri and me to make sure we hadn't *ever* wandered too close to the Doove.

Mother had believed that satisfying genuine curiosity kept children out of trouble. She was always one for the brutal truth. She answered our questions about the forest openly, even to the point of scaring us with myths and monsters.

I could still hear her voice, "The Fear Dorca haunts the Doove, my beautiful girls. He's no one to mess with. He does the evil fairy queen's bidding, and her bidding is *never* good. The Dark Man is her right-hand man in the Unseelie Court, a darkling so ominous and deadly it's been said he's death personified. He moves in the shadows so smoothly some say he *is* shadows.

"If he catches a human in the forest, he will snatch them away to the Unseelie Court to be used for the queen's amusement. We all know what happened to Tamlane so many years ago. Disappeared, never to be seen again. And all the young men after him? Turned to monsters fated to roam the Doove forever.

"Promise me, both of you, that you will never, *ever* take so much as one tiny baby step into the Doove." She had pinned us with a look overflowing with love and worry.

I could hear my childish reply echo through the years, "Not even if we're being chased by a bad man or a witch?"

"Or a monster," Catri had added with wide eyes.

"Not even then." Mother looked grim. "Better to die quickly at the hands of man than to be at the mercy of the Unseelie Court."

Looking back, it was hard to tell whether she spoke from experience or hearsay. It didn't matter. She was deadly serious.

I was breaking my promise to her now, and it grieved me. I was a woman of my word and took my oaths seriously. But I had to fulfill another vow I'd made to her as I sat next to her on her deathbed, watching her slowly, painfully waste away and die.

"Catri is weak and sick." Mother clutched my hand weakly and looked at me beseechingly with sunken eyes, her face pale. "You must take care of her while she lives, which won't be much longer. At the rapid rate she's aging, I thought I would outlive her."

Mother squeezed my hand. "I hate to burden you, my strong girl. You have your whole life in front of you and youth is fleeting, not something to ever be squandered. I want you to be able to live your life to the fullest, not spend it taking care of a girl who's an old woman before her time." Her voice broke. I knew how much she loved Catri, too. We both wished things were different. "But soon enough, you'll be free. Promise?"

"I'd never abandon Catri, Mother. You can count on me."

Mother leaned back. Her voice was barely a whisper, "If only there were a way to break the curse."

"I'll find it. I'll *find* a way." My impetuous nature had always gotten the better of me, made me overconfident. But one had to believe or why even try?

"Oh, Maisie, my innocent." Mother reached up and stroked my cheek. "Never promise something that's beyond your control."

I set my jaw, determined not to let either of them down. "Then I can only promise that I'll try. With all my body and soul. I promise I'll do my best."

So here I was, doing my best. Breaking one promise while trying to keep another.

I picked my way through the maze of underbrush. The

darkness had washed all traces of autumn color away, but fallen leaves and moist muck covered the forest floor.

The musty, earthy scent of decaying plant life filled the air. Ancient oaks and ash rustled above me. I lived in fear of stepping on another twig and sending an explosion of sound through the forest again, pointing directly toward me a second time. I wished I was lighter of foot. There was no need to hand myself to the Fear Dorca so easily. Or alert my competition from the village to my location.

The relative quiet meant that either I didn't have company, or someone had learned to move with more stealth than was humanly possible. I suppressed a shiver at the thought. Darklings moved like mist and shadow.

I was on a hunt for healing for Catri. Everyone else in the village and surrounding province was on a hunt for beauty. Beauty was the coin of the realm in the kingdom and our province was sadly lacking in it, according to worldly standards, at least. We had our own touchstones, but those wouldn't please the king. And *everyone* knew it.

Beauty brought with it great power and wealth. No more so than now when *so* much was at stake. *For everyone.* Someone *would be* queen.

It was unfortunate timing that Catri's illness had driven me to Maurelle for help at the same time our handsome young king announced he was in need of a bride and our province was next on his list to choose one from. Worse luck that the rose appeared to be the solution for all of us. More competition and danger for me, as if there wasn't enough already. Although, with the value of beauty so high, at any time I would have competition for something more valuable than gold.

"Beauty is always youth," Maurelle had said to me in her dark cottage full of the jars and unctions of her trade. "And youthful beauty is always a sign of good health. A beauty potion will cure Catri. I can assure you of that."

I couldn't argue with her logic. Common sense is common sense. When was the last time I'd heard an attractive older woman called beautiful without "for her age" added on? Beauty had to be youth. And the blush of youth was only beautiful when accompanied by fine health. Villagers had been going to Maurelle for beauty potions as long as I could remember. Why hadn't I thought of it before?

It was as if Maurelle read my mind, "Don't blame yourself for not coming to me earlier with this idea. I couldn't have helped you before. Without the rose, there isn't a potion strong enough. All the rest of my concoctions are only creams and lotions that aid or enhance beauty. They can't create it out of whole cloth. They can't reverse the aging process."

I would have bet my life that Maurelle had promised too many others that a potion made from the rose would solve their problems, as she had me, and sent them after it as well. People with power and influence, and much heavier purses than mine. Rumors of it had even reached our home on the outskirts of civilization.

As much as she'd tried to hide it, Maurelle had reeked of desperation. She wanted, *needed*, that rose. Even her long nose had broken out with sweat. I'd never seen her so agitated. The more people she sent out, the greater the chance that one of us would succeed in the nearly impossible task. Success was theoretically possible, but it certainly wasn't probable.

I couldn't blame her. I would have used that logic if I were her, too. But in the name of her own interests, she'd pitted us against each other, making competitors and enemies of neighbors and friends.

The stakes were high, and the villagers had never been my friends. I was the strange girl from the strange family that lived on the edge of the Doove, a misfit among misfits. I was a girl without a beauty mark—a missing arm or a too-short leg, too many fingers or toes, the complete lack of ears, or an extra limb, something to mark my family as having served honorably in the Great Magic War and been cursed for it. Something that made me unique and, more often than not, resulted in a special talent.

I wasn't ugly by any means. But I was certainly no beauty. In any case, not beautiful enough to catch a king's eye and right now, that was all that mattered to everyone but me.

How hard was I prepared to fight my own people for the rose? Weren't we all supposed to be on the same side? I couldn't allow myself to dwell on the thought of what I might, or might not, do, or have to do, and the consequences of either choice.

Even if I succeeded, I didn't trust Maurelle not to double-cross me. I worried that *if* I managed to bring her the rose, she wouldn't uphold her end of our bargain.

I was growing warier by the moment. I should have seen *someone* else in pursuit of rose magic, too, by now. If I was on the right track, and the rose was nearby, shouldn't there be scores of others ready to fight for it? How sure was Maurelle of the location of the rose? Was she hedging her bets? Sending each of us to a place she only *hoped* it would be? Had she sent me to the least likely spot while she sent a higher bidder to a glen she was more confident in? I had nothing to offer her but my desperation to save my sister and my willingness to brave the forest. Others had far more.

I clenched the iron dagger tighter.

Maurelle's warning kept echoing back. *Find the rose, catch it as it blooms at the peak light of the blue moon, cut it, and get out of the forest as fast as your feet can carry you. Don't worry about a light. The rose will guide you out.*

I was already doubting the directions she'd given me. I was far deeper into the forest than she'd led me to believe the rose would be. Either I was lost, or Maurelle had downplayed just how dangerously deep into the forest the rose was. But my memory was good. I was sure I was following her correctly. And I hadn't yet missed a single one of the markers she'd told me to look for. But what if I were running behind?

I had to hurry. I wanted plenty of time to get in position.

The forest floor was a tangle of grasping, grabbing fallen trees, branches, twigs, and limbs determined, each in their own way, to slow me down. Twigs snagged my stockings and skirts. Branches threatened my footing. Heaving roots made the ground uneven and tricky to cover quickly without tripping. If I fell and sprained an ankle, no one would come looking for me.

Everything here loved the darkness and decorated itself according to those tastes. Moss, lichen, fungi and mushrooms covered thick tree trunks like finery. Mushrooms grew thickly on the ground, nurtured by decaying leaves.

The darkness, as it fell, seemed almost alive. My mother's words of warning rang in my ears. "Darklings are as stealth as darkness itself, moving without sound."

The dew had already fallen. I could see my breath. At home, breath floated and coiled until it evaporated into thin strands into the air and disappeared. Here, it lay flat and heavy, reflecting even the smallest amount of light, pointing to me. I thought it odd that I saw no one else's breath hanging on the air.

I wore my heaviest cloak, but still I shivered. Overhead, the ancient oaks and ash strangled all but the most determined strands of moonlight. Despite Maurelle's warning, I had a candle in my pocket. If necessary, I *would* use it. After all, it was a universal truth that even the smallest prick of light could overwhelm darkness. And then I would take my chances.

I cursed myself for letting desperation rule my head. I reached a glen. This had to be it. Just as Maurelle had described, before me stood a giant ash tree, its trunk covered in a distinctive pattern of mushrooms that looked like handles beckoning me to climb the tree.

"Don't touch them," Maurelle had warned. "They're poisonous to the touch, like poison ivy or stinging nettle. But a *thousand* times worse. They're your sign. The rose will be in the small clearing just past the tree."

Too afraid to step into the open, I pushed some foliage aside and crouched behind a clump of bushes as I peered into the clearing, looking for my floral quarry.

My pulse panicked in my ears. The rose was *nowhere* in sight.

I cursed my foolishness. I never should have trusted Maurelle. Or been out on what was ostensibly *my* mission but was more than likely *hers* and hers *alone*. *Never trust a witch* was the second rule my mother had taught me.

The moon disappeared behind a cloud. The last of the light flickered out. I was thrown into utter, complete darkness. My heart raced. My skin crawled. I was overwhelmed with a sense of being closed in and suffocated. If Maurelle was wrong that the night would be clear, and that cloud persisted...

Just as I reached for the candle in my pocket, a beam of blue light cut through the canopy overhead. The moonbeam was so bright and clear that it lit the surrounding trees and underbrush until I could see the bright reds and oranges of the most spectacular of fall foliage.

But the rose? Where is the rose?

I looked around frantically. *No rosebush. No rose.*

Anger. Betrayal. Abject fear. So many emotions that had no names.

Had I made a mistake, or had Maurelle intentionally sent me to my death?

A wisp of fog appeared from deep in the woods across the glen from me. It curled its way into the glen, growing denser and thicker as it moved and filled the clearing.

The forest is fighting back against the light. I shuddered, not daring to wager on which would win. But I had a sinking feeling.

But the moonlight persisted, lighting the fog blue, caressing it until it glowed. And then, out of the moist compost on the forest floor, a small cane of a rosebush pushed up. Just one cane. It sprouted one leaf, then two as it grew at an enchanted, accelerated rate before my eyes. A bud grew out of one end, producing one long-stemmed deep red rose. As the fog grew denser, the bud began opening.

Magically, the light of the blue moon cut the fog completely in two, parting it so that the rose stood in a clear, dancing moonbeam.

I gasped as the bud opened into one perfect, dazzling blood red rose.

I had never seen anything so beautiful and perfect. The light sparkled on the petals as if lighting up dew. But the dew had long since settled. Nothing but magic explained the sparkles.

I stared, mesmerized. How could I cut something that beautiful off from its lifeblood?

I swore that the rose turned in my direction and bowed ever so slightly on its stem as if giving me a nod of its head.

I can't kill something so beautiful and alive.

My hands shook. I hesitated and swallowed hard.

In that instant, the moon began to dip in the sky. The fog sensed its weakness, gained strength, and began breaching the moonbeam's defenses.

I had no time to think. I gripped my dagger tightly, stepped into the clearing, and lunged for the rose.

CHAPTER 2
THE ROSE CALLS

Only my love for my sister could have forced me into the clearing where I was an open target for any of the monsters in the forest. Only the thought of saving Catri's life could have given me the courage to reach past the sparks and sparkles surrounding the enchanted rose, kneel in the damp dirt, and grab its stem at the base. Only for my sister would I have risked it all.

I grabbed the stem of the rose with my left hand, careful to avoid thorns, and wielded my dagger in my right. The moment I touched the rose, a thousand images of beauty coursed through me, filling me with a wonderful awe. Things I had never seen. Things I could never have imagined—fields of gold and jewels. Waterfalls lit in pinks and purples. Sunsets lit like rainbows. Flowers beautiful enough to take my breath away. Faces of beautiful people, so perfect, that they couldn't have been from this world. A sense of perfect love that made me want to cry with joy.

There was power here. *Immense power.* I never wanted to let go. But even though my senses were overwhelmed with beauty in all of its forms, I still had enough common sense to realize that a prize this valuable and powerful could be dangerous in *anyone's* hands, but especially in those of a witch. At the same time, my doubts that this rose could make Catri young again and beautiful, too, vanished. If only *I* knew how to use it. Yet how could I cut it?

Darkness and fog were fast closing in around me. With tears streaming down my face, I pictured Catri's face and slid my dagger into the flesh of the rose cane, near the ground to make sure I got the most stem.

From Maurelle's warning, I expected to have to work harder to cut through the cane of the bush. But I was strong and used to hard work and my dagger was sharp. It cut through the cane in a single, vicious slice. The moment the rose came free in my hand, the beautiful images vanished. The overwhelming joyful feeling of love evaporated. The connection was broken. I was left with only my mortal human love for my sister. But the rose still sparkled. It still had power.

I bowed my head, apologizing silently to the rose for taking it. *Your life and magic aren't for me. I'm not that selfish. I have no need of them. You give your essence for my sister. She's worth everything. Your sacrifice isn't in vain.*

I closed my eyes and inhaled deeply, hoping the scent would bring the connection to beauty back. Its fragrance was like nothing I'd ever breathed before, heavenly perfume, rose perfection, untainted with any hint of mildew or decay. Nothing that interfered with its essence

and bouquet. Old ladies give the scent of rose a bad reputation as belonging to the ancient, but this scent was so
youthful it was almost eternal.

I smiled to myself, happy for the first time in ages.
Amazed that I could feel joyful in this frightening deep
darkness.

Out of nowhere, without making a sound to announce
itself, something slammed into my left hand with brutal,
wicked force. The impact knocked my arm outward away
from my body. My hand reflexively uncurled, losing its
grip on the rose.

I screamed. My eyes flew open in time to see the rose
flying in an arc away from me. I watched its trajectory into
the heart of the foggy glen in horror. It landed too far away
for me to reach, still glowing, lighting the fog even more
brilliant blue. The fog seemed to have a life of its own. It
closed in on the rose, trying to snuff out the light.

I doubled over, cradling my hand in my lap helplessly.
It was useless. I couldn't move my fingers. I couldn't move,
period. The pain, and the shock, were so excruciating that
they took my breath away.

The darkness seemed to close in and dance around me.
A shadow here on one side of me, then on the other as if
studying me from all angles. This darkness was alive, and
it was toying with me. Trying to terrify me. I didn't want
to tell it, but it needn't have tried so hard. I was already
petrified.

If I were going to survive, I had to get the rose back
while it still glowed and get out of the clearing.

I fought nausea. Cold sweat broke out on my brow. My
stomach heaved. I swallowed hard against it, trying not to

show just how terrified and helpless I was. I silently prayed for something, *anything*, to save me. Where were those infamous marauding Doove bear when I needed them?

Something landed with a bush-shaking thud to my right, just in front of me in the clearing. I jumped, startled, and winced with pain. But I dared not look.

However, the dark, heatless presence that stood over me seemed amused.

I had been avoiding the darkness's gaze, but if I were going to fight, I needed to size up my opponent. I swallowed hard and looked up into the face of the most dangerously gorgeous man I had ever seen. It was a dark and vicious beauty, cold to its core, but nonetheless stunning. He was tall and perfectly proportioned, with broad shoulders that spoke of great strength.

It was hard to explain how I could see him in the darkness, but the fact that he almost absorbed light seemed to make it possible. He was clad immaculately in expensive black leather and decorated with black jewels—diamonds and onyx—that seemed not to reflect the light, but rather trap it. His clothing befit high-ranking nobility. He was dressed for battle. His eyes were equally dark and soulless, but magnetic at the same time. To my horror, I felt them sucking at the last of my warmth.

Somehow, I managed to hang onto the dagger in my right hand.

"Thief." His voice was deep and seductive, mesmerizing, even as it accused me. It was almost as if he were issuing me a compliment.

It wasn't until he spoke that I realized he was winged.

He walked around me, spreading his large, black, sparkling wings as if to further intimidate me. As if he were playing with a mouse.

He needn't have bothered. I was already immobilized with fear.

He moved like smoke and shadow. Which explained how he'd sneaked up on me without making a sound in the first place. He clearly wasn't human. I might have been happy for that, given other circumstances. On the bright side, at least one of the very human villagers hadn't just outplayed me for the rose.

The bushes nearby rattled again. Without thinking, I turned toward them. The source of the thud became obvious. A breathtaking young man lay on the ground. He had pushed up into an awkward sitting position. He was also exceptionally well built and dressed richly in gear appropriate for a high-ranking official or soldier. But there was much more than dark and smoke to him. He was alive with warmth and heat and substance.

The rose's glow lit him in a flattering, golden light, doing its best to hide the bruising and swelling from a vicious beating that had apparently been interrupted when he thudded into my glen. His left eye was swelling shut. His lip was fat, and blood ran from his nose. He wiped the blood with his sleeve and rose to a stand.

He's beautiful.

Maybe that was the rose talking. Or maybe it was me talking to myself. But somehow, I knew it to be true. I'd never seen such a perfectly formed man before. Which, yes, I lived in the land of misfits, but even still...

Our eyes met. The heat of his gaze spread over me, reaching to my most intimate areas.

An emotional jolt and connection so shocking and strong it felt almost physical rocked me back. It must have been the shock I was in, but it was almost as if I could read his mind.

"Run!" He lunged for the dark man.

This was my chance to escape, and I was grateful for it. But I couldn't leave without that rose. Without it, I was doomed to die in the forest. Maybe I was doomed, anyway.

The winged darkling focused on the handsome injured man. While the darkling's attention was diverted, I pushed to a stand and made a dash for the rose.

But the darkling wasn't intimidated by either of us. He calmly knocked back my would-be rescuer with a flick of his wrist, sending him sprawling without touching him. The darkling moved like the fog itself to the rose and ground it into the ground with his heel. He may have moved like mist, but he definitely had power and might and material form. The rose lay bruised beneath his feet.

"No!" I lunged for him.

The young man scrambled to his feet. With one hand, the dark fae held him back, squeezing his throat with an invisible grip. With the other, he swatted me away as if I were as inconsequential as gossamer.

The light of the rose had dimmed, but it still flickered. I hadn't come this far to be defeated. I sprawled on the ground, dazed, pretending to have fainted, hoping the winged creature would lose interest in me while he toyed with the other man, and I thought up a plan.

The injured man was gasping. My eyes were closed, but I was tortured by the terrible rattling as he struggled to breath.

The darkling must have tightened his grip. The gasping grew more desperate.

"Give it up. The Queen wants you alive, more's the pity. For you. As long as I deliver you still breathing, I can torture you all I like. She didn't specify *how* intact you have to be when I deliver you. Or how pretty." His laugh was low and seductive despite the wickedness he was inflicting. He seemed genuinely amused. However, he was the only one among us who found the situation funny. "A quick death would be easier and more merciful, believe me."

Something in me snapped. I weighed the odds and realized that either way fate favored me dying. Either at the hands of this dark fae or lost wandering in the woods. Maybe the darkling was right—better a quick death at his hand, he hadn't promised me I'd live, than a slow death in the forest.

Another violent gasp wrenched my heart. I couldn't shake our connection. I couldn't push his bruised face out of my mind. I couldn't make myself so selfish that I would let him suffer without trying to help him.

I lost my temper, and with it, my sense of fear. Mother had taught me it was better to go down fighting than willingly accept death at another's hand. At best, I hoped to free the other man. He, at least, had a chance at life.

Talk, talk all you like, darkling. Keep making your little speech.

I clenched the dagger so tightly my fingers ached in

the cold. I'd only have one chance. I opened my eyes just a crack, mentally measured the distance, weighed the long odds, pushed myself up with my elbow, and sprung to my feet.

Never underestimate the element of surprise. I caught the darkling off guard. Unfortunately, not off guard *enough*. Just as my dagger met the soft flesh of his bare neck, he caught my hand.

Our eyes met. His flamed with fury.

I was sure I was dead. I'd barely nicked him. A small trickle of dark, nearly black, blood ran down his neck.

His eyes went wide. He dropped my hand and slapped his hand over the small cut on his neck. "Witch." A flap of his wings and he disappeared like a shadow.

Shaking and stunned, I fell to the ground, protecting my injured hand in my lap and breathing hard. I wasn't sure what had just happened. I turned to my companion. "Are you all right?"

He rubbed his throat. "I'll survive. Thanks to you." His voice was scratchy. "What about you?"

"I'm alive."

He nodded grimly. "Aye." He handed me the rose. "I believe this belongs to you."

For some reason, I reached for it with my left hand. Maybe because my right was still clutching the dagger and I couldn't make myself loosen my grip. It took all my resolve to move two of my fingers enough through the pain to grasp the rose.

As I turned to thank him, he cocked his head, listening to something I couldn't hear. "You have to get out of the forest." He shoved me down and pushed me into the bushes. "*Hide.*"

Before I could respond, a pair of fae appeared on either side of him. I hunkered down in my hiding spot, hiding the rose beneath my cloak. The pair grabbed him beneath his arms and pulled him roughly to his feet while he struggled against them. With a rustle of wings, they disappeared with him, leaving a trail of sparkles in their wake.

I stared open-mouthed at the space where he had been just moments before. I was devastated and heartbroken. How often did one encounter such beauty *anywhere*, but especially in this remote part of the world? Or such self-sacrifice?

I felt an overwhelming sense of guilt. I'd cowered. Just left him to his fate. Even though any attempt on my part would have most likely been futile, and I had Catri to think about, shame wouldn't leave me alone.

He wanted to save me, wanted me to hide and stay hidden.

Mother had taught me to accept gifts with good grace. He'd known they were coming for him and sought to spare me, that much was clear. But my actions still didn't sit right with my conscience. *Coward.*

It did no good to dwell on it now. This was no place to linger.

I pulled the rose out from beneath my cloak. It was crushed and wilting fast. Missing many of its petals. Maurelle had said it would lead me out of the forest. When I'd asked how, she'd simply reiterated that it would.

Looking at it now, I wondered how. And whether it had enough strength left to do the job.

It was freezing in the woods. Even the fingers on my

good hand were growing stiff. I pulled my gloves from my cloak pocket and, wincing, managed to gingerly pull them on over my battered fingers, hoping the gloves would protect the rose and preserve its remaining magic as well as keep me warm.

How *do* you talk to a rose?

I decided to try the lighthearted approach. I looked it directly in its remaining petals. Its poor bud head drooped terribly. "Well, are you going to sit there wilting? Or are you going to get us out of here before the next set of evil fae arrive?"

I caught one of its petals as it fell and fluttered toward the ground. I put it gently in my pocket. "I'll just keep this safe for you. In all seriousness, dear rose, I'd appreciate your help. Point the way and I'll carry you out of here. I'll take good care of you, I promise."

One side of the rose sparkled and shot out a beam of light in one direction as if pointing the way. Since being hit by the darkling, I was totally disoriented. I had no idea which direction I'd come from, or where the village lay. I was at the rose's mercy. I hoped it had a better sense of direction than I did.

"I guess I'll have to trust you."

CHAPTER 3
OUT OF THE DOOVE

B y the time I broke out of the Doove into the clearing near home, my pocket was full of petals and my left hand was numb. I had been as gentle as I could, but the rose wasn't much more than a broken green rosehip on a battered stem now. I could only hope I'd caught all the petals as they'd fallen, and not missed one. As far as I could tell now that we were in the light, the rose was no longer sparkling.

Dawn had broken. The sun was rising and stirring the frosty fields to mist. The long night full of beauty and terror was behind me.

I still held my dagger in my right hand and the rose in my left. I was exhausted, hungry, parched with thirst. But so grateful to be alive, and out of the forest, that I nearly fell to my knees and cried, even though home was in sight.

I simply had to keep putting one foot in front of the other. Unfortunately, Maurelle's carriage blocked my path.

23

I hadn't expected to see *her* here. And she, apparently, hadn't expected to see me, either. Her eyebrows shot up as she looked down at me from on high in the carriage box.

I'd never been good at reading her thoughts. She always kept them close. I must have really shocked her if her eyebrows had gotten away from her this time.

Betting on someone else's success? I thought, though there was no one else around. And I hadn't encountered another human in the forest, either.

Her gaze fell greedily on the length of rose stem visible in my gloved hand.

She gathered her voluminous black skirts and hopped down from her seat in the carriage. "Maisie Jayne Rose, the young woman who survived a night in the Doove." Her voice dripped false honey and sweetness, reflecting only palely the light of the sunrise as she complimented me.

Maurelle had the ability to bounce light in voice, expression, and thought, but it never emanated directly from her. And because it was *only* an imitation, it rang false.

She didn't fool me. I cradled the remains of the rose closer, holding my information tightly, too. Could I convince her, or trick her, if necessary, into working with a broken rose? I'd have to try.

"You'll be forever famous. Immortalized in folk song and story." She held out her hand. "You have the rose?"

I clutched what was left of the rose as tightly as my bruised fingers would let me, hiding the broken bud from her. "I do. It was hard won. I need your promise that you will only use it for Catri."

Her eyes flashed. "I agreed to use the rose to help your sister. That was the bargain."

She'd sidestepped the issue, which told me all I needed to know. She couldn't be trusted. It was clear she was trying to project that she held all the power in this negotiation. But I held the rose and that gave me power, too.

I stared her down. "The king wants a beautiful wife, *the* most beautiful wife in the land. Every unmarried woman in the province wants to be that most beautiful person. Beauty, in this case, means power and great wealth."

"You're not telling me anything I, or any of us, don't know, Maisie." Her smile was patronizing, but her voice was calm, and as mesmerizing as a spinning top. She had age and experience on me, as well as her skill with spells and potions and trances. I would have to step carefully.

"Why are we wasting time discussing the king's love life?" She laid a hand gently on my arm and crooned in my ear, "The sooner I have the rose, the sooner I can start the potion and we can heal Catri."

I felt my defenses dropping. *You want to help Catri. Give her the rose.* The words appeared in my mind, but they weren't in my voice. My hand suddenly developed a mind of its own, unfurling in preparation for handing Maurelle the rose.

The rose stem slid through my loosened grip. On its way down, a thorn caught my glove and pricked me through it, breaking the trance. *She's inside your head. Push her out.*

I grasped the rose just in time, letting the thorn dig into my flesh, hoping the pain would keep me out of the spell of her trance. Anything to keep myself alert and clear-headed. I had love for my sister on my side, and I had seen the true power of the flower and faced death. I wouldn't allow Maurelle to steal from me. "The king's desire makes the rose and any beauty potion you make from it priceless."

Maurelle's eyes narrowed. She knew I spoke truth and had caught her in her plans. She dropped her hand from my arm.

I wasn't the easy, gullible prey she'd been expecting from our first meeting. She hadn't counted on my experience in the Doove stealing my naiveté.

I'd gone to her desperate to find a cure for my dying sister. Maurelle had surprised me by claiming that a beauty potion *would* heal, and cure, Catri completely. And that there was a rose that she needed for just such a potion. And with the king looking for a beautiful wife from our province...

"It's only valuable *to me* because you say your beauty potion can reverse Catri's aging sickness," I said. "I don't care about beauty like the others do. Neither Catri, nor I do. I just want her healthy. She has no desire to be the queen."

That wasn't exactly true. I couldn't speak to whether Catri wanted to be beautiful. Maybe she did. And who could blame her after the taunting she'd received since her sickness first appeared? But *I* certainly did not. Nor did I want to be queen. Anyway, that was a moot point. This potion wasn't *for* me.

If the potion not only healed Catri, but made her beautiful, and she wanted to be queen, I would try to talk her out of it. Better to marry a kinder man that would treat her well than sit in the callous seat of power. It was an open secret that our young, handsome king was a ruthless man. This marriage was not only being forced on him, but by law, he was required to choose a bride from our territory of the flawed and unbeautiful. We were the place where the defective, those not beautiful or perfect enough for the Royal Circle, were sent. He could hardly be happy about it.

"I want a double portion of the potion, enough so that if Catri needs a second dose down the road, I'll have it on hand. And I want my portion first, with enough time to see whether it's going to work or not before we let any of it go. After that, you're free to sell it to whomever you want for whatever price."

Maurelle's expression was placid, but her eyes flashed. She didn't like fair bargains, but even she could see I wasn't backing down. "I always guarantee my work. Just wait until you see with your own eyes how young and healthy your sister becomes. Health is beauty, after all." She held out her hand again.

As I slowly produced the rose, my heart hammered.

When she saw its battered condition, rage replaced the reflected light in her eyes.

I took a step back, afraid she would strike me.

"I told you to bring it to me *intact*." Her voice was like dark water, deep and icy.

I lifted my chin. "Can I help it if the Fear Dorca ground it into the dirt with his heel before my very eyes? You should thank me and be grateful I was able to save *any* part of it. I rescued it from Death."

Maurelle leaned away from me as if suddenly afraid.

"The Fear Dorca touched it?" She took a step back.

I nodded.

She paused and studied me intently. "You're lying."

I narrowed my eyes at her and pulled up my hand holding the dagger. I wasn't exactly threatening her, more showing her I didn't like being accused of being false.

She softened her tone. "Or you're mistaken. You're tired. Anyone in your condition can be forgiven for making a mistake. The Doove makes the best of us imagine things. Maybe you saw a bear, or a cougar. No one sees the Fear Dorca and lives to return to the mortal realm."

"He was a darkling with black wings that spanned the glen. He moved like shadow and smoke, so dark he was almost darkness itself. He was dressed in black jewels like a nobleman. And he spoke of *his* queen." I purposefully omitted the handsome stranger from my story. The memory of him belonged to me alone.

Maurelle paled. "What was *he* doing in the glen?"

"Protecting the rose," I lied.

Maurelle whispered an incantation of some kind and circled herself with two fingers. "If that's true, the rose is of no use to me now. The Fear Dorca brings only death, not beauty." Her eyes narrowed. "I can't believe you survived him."

I ignored her jibe. She could believe what she wanted. "What you say can't be true. He was beautiful, truly, the most darkly beautiful male I've ever looked upon."

Her eyes went wide with fear as if she suddenly believed that I had seen the *real* Fear Dorca, not a figment of my own imagination. I had only figured out who the darkling had to be myself as I ran through the forest.

28

Maurelle had just confirmed my suspicions. Most people believed the Fear Dorca was a hideous creature, so ugly even The Outlands would reject him. Statues mocking him, strategically placed to ward him off, portrayed him as scaled and horned.

"Get rid of it. If he touched it, it will only bring curses from here out." Maurelle backed into her carriage. "The potion only works with a complete, *perfect* rose."

"That's impossible." I held my ground. "Nothing is perfect." But even as I spoke, I knew the rose had been perfect when it first bloomed.

I held the stem out to Maurelle. "There must be *something* you can do with it? Make a potion that would slow Catri's aging, even that would be something. Give me a little more time to figure out a plan." I hated pleading with her.

Maurelle's gaze ran along the stem. She looked regretful, but afraid. And there was an undertone of anger, but I sensed it wasn't at me. I was only the unfortunate soul near enough to direct it to. "*No.* Take it away from me. Take it *away.*"

"But what should I do with it? Maybe another witch—"

"No one will touch it. You'd be best off burying it. Somewhere far away from hallowed ground where you can't disturb the dead." She slithered into the box of her carriage, snapped the reins, and rattled off.

What did I do? All of this for nothing? I wanted to lie down and cry. But what good would that do? I had to get home. Catri would be up soon and worry if I didn't come home.

Maybe Ree would have an idea. He was generally useless unless he was up to no good. But he even though he was only an exotic brownie from the south, a house fae, he was connected to the fae world.

Catri was at the stove, stirring a pot of porridge when I stumbled in. It broke my heart to see her stooped and stiff, her young head gray. Every move was a labor for her.

"You're back." She lifted the pot off the stove and set it on the table. "Just in time for breakfast." Her tone was sweet, but full of relief. She was seldom accusing.

Breakfast was always porridge. Sometimes with a little bacon, if we were very lucky. Today, just porridge.

"You shouldn't have gone, but I knew you would. You've always been fearless and stubborn. I would have stopped you if I could." She paused.

We both knew she was too feeble to physically restrain me. At one time, she might have been able to tug at my heartstrings with her pleas. But things were too desperate now. Even a few weeks ago, I might have worried about what would happen to her if I failed and was killed or abducted in the forest. But now she was declining so quickly that death was inevitable sooner rather than later. Ree, for all of his southern tendencies, would have taken care of her until the end.

"I made enough breakfast for two, hoping you'd make it back." Her voice cracked with emotion. That was Catri, selfless. She didn't even ask about the rose. She certainly didn't lead with it.

There was no need to keep her in suspense. I set the battered rose on the table.

She stared at it. "That's *it*? *That's* the priceless rose?"

"The very one. But Maurelle wouldn't take it." I reached for a bowl.

"*What?*"

I shook my head. "Never trust a witch."

I pulled the rose petals from my cloak pocket and filled the bowl with them. "It's not exactly intact, as she requested. But I have all the pieces. One would think that if they're going into a potion anyway, it would make no difference to the finished product whether they go in as a whole or not."

I set my dagger down and pulled off my gloves, right hand first, then reached for the left, bracing myself for the inevitable pain. Remarkably, the left glove slid off with no trouble, causing not even a pang. I didn't even notice until the glove was off that the thorn was still obviously sticking out. It hadn't even scratched me as I'd removed the glove.

As I held my hand out and stretched my fingers, Catri gasped. "Maisie! *Your hand.*" She pointed.

I was already staring at it and flexing it. All of the pain was gone. "It's healed."

"What?" She looked suddenly worried. "*Healed?* Was it injured?" She took a stiff step closer.

I nodded. "Badly. In the forest." I would have to be careful how I told her the story. *Later.* "But look at it now."

"It's beautiful." She took my hand in her bony, wrinkled ones. "So soft and smooth. It's perfect. Your pointer finger is no longer turned in. Your scars and callouses are gone. Your fingers are long and perfectly shaped. Even your fingernails are pink and lovely, with perfect half-moons showing."

Catri was trying hard not to show it, but envy seeped into her voice. She had always loved beautiful things. She'd been such a pretty, precocious child, far prettier than me. Before the aging sickness manifested in her, everyone had conceded that she would be the beauty of the province.

My hands had always been perfectly functional, but never beautiful. My nails were always chipped and ugly from the hard work of running our small croft.

I stared down at my left hand and compared it to my right. Not only had it healed, but it was now a perfect version of itself. I had been certain that the very tip of the thorn had broken off into my hand and that I would have to dig it out like a sliver. But there was no sign of it now.

I grabbed my glove and pulled the thorn from it—yes, the tip was missing. Maybe I'd been mistaken about it digging into my skin. Maybe it had brushed off. On any account, I was glad I wouldn't have to try to dig it out.

I held my hands out in front of me again, comparing them side by side, stunned. I flexed my fingers. My hand moved as gracefully as it was beautiful. There was no pain, just fluid movement.

I turned to my sister, shaking with excitement. "You know what this means?"

She stared back at me wide-eyed and mute.

"We don't need Maurelle!" I could barely contain myself. "We never *did*, and she knew it. The rose can heal you all by itself!"

CHAPTER 4
DARK MAGIC

Before Catri could respond, the pot of porridge tipped over on the table behind us. We both jumped and spun around.

Her reactions were slow. She reached for it.

My reactions were faster. I grabbed the hot pot with my glove and managed to right it before more than a dribble of porridge spilled out. "Ree!" I waggled my finger at the tiny house fae standing next to it.

Gabriele Antonio D'Amicco, or Ree, as we called him, stood on the table, with a spoon that was nearly as tall as he was, scooping up the porridge greedily. "What? Am I not part of this family? Do you expect me to go hungry? I need food to keep up my impressive strength." He flexed a muscle.

Always trying to impress.

"It's breakfast time, isn't it? This body doesn't run on empty." He winked impishly. He was such a comical little flirt.

"You could have asked for a serving like a normal person," I said.

Ree puffed out his chest. "I'm no normal person, as you say. I'm a *munacielli* of the highest order. A prince among his people..."

Catri spoke to me in an aside past her cupped hand, "Ree's here?"

I nodded. It was a puzzle to both of us, but she had never been able to see him. Whereas I *always* had from earliest memory. She used to accuse me of having an imaginary friend, but eventually came to believe that Ree was real. Now she had to rely on my eyes and accounts of him. "And up to his antics," I replied out of the side of my mouth.

I somehow managed to resist rolling my eyes, but it was hard to keep a straight face. We'd heard this speech too many times before. Me, firsthand, and Catri in my relating it to her. "He's giving the speech," I whispered to her.

I couldn't help interrupting his diatribe, "I thought house fae were supposed to be heard, at most, but never seen." I shouldn't have teased Ree, knowing I would rile him up.

"That's only for amateurs. Those of low birth." He took a slurp of porridge. "If more of us showed ourselves, more of your kind would believe we were real, not just myths, and treat us with more respect. We could get more credit, rather than be blamed for minor mishaps that are beneath our dignity."

"Then why don't you show yourself to Catri?" It seemed like a reasonable question to me.

34

Ree shrugged. "We've been over this before. She could see me if she truly believed and wanted to. I'm not hiding."

I let out a sigh. Of course, Catri believed. But I wasn't going to argue the point with Ree again.

"You get too much credit as it is," I said, dryly. "People ascribe credit to you for every setback, small *and* large, when most of them are simply accidents. In my opinion, your reputation for mischief is greatly *enhanced* by your fellow fae remaining in the shadows."

I pulled out a chair at the table across from him and collapsed into it.

For my entire life, at least the part that I could remember, we had been cursed, or honored, depending on how you looked at it, with a house fae from the south instead of a native friendly northern one. The cultural differences between the two were extreme.

Northern house fae, brownies, could be mischievous and surly, sure. But they were generally helpful. A family could count on them, often in surprising ways, in times of real emergencies. I, myself, knew at least half a dozen families that swore their house fae had rendered them invaluable services. In one case, even going out in a blizzard and bringing back the midwife to save a mother in labor and her baby. The master of the house was so grateful, he gave the brownie a valuable coat.

Southern house fae typically lived in the warm, sunny regions in and around the Royal Circle. By reputation, they were notorious pranksters and hoarders of pots of gold. They delighted in annoying the households they occupied and were highly unreliable, rarely, if ever, helping in times of need. Given how privileged and wealthy the south was, particularly the Royal Circle, northerners generally approved of the average southern house fae's behavior. The nobles and royals deserved *some* adversity, even if it *was* minor compared to our struggles.

Such was our misfit life that Ree had adopted us, following us wherever we moved. He never explained why *he*, apparently a house fae of noble birth, had chosen to leave his native lands. Instead, he complained about our climate, food, and culture. We were left to assume he was a misfit of some kind, too, and had been banished to the north to our province of the misfit and malformed. Whatever the case, we were unable to shake him. Mother had given up long ago.

He was off on another tear, spouting his speech between slurps of porridge. I sat silently shaking with my hand over my mouth, trying to hold my laughter in. Catri focused her gaze where I did, politely silent although she couldn't see or hear him.

I finally interrupted him again. "How is it that you can sneak up on us like that?"

"Years of training and experience. I'm older than I look." He ran his hand through his hair and preened exaggeratedly. I could never tell whether he was serious when he did this or just trying to get a laugh out of me.

I had no idea how old Ree really was, but he certainly looked young, no older than me. I would say no older than Catri *and* me, but, of course, Catri looked decades and decades older than she actually was.

Ree was dark-haired and dark-eyed. He could change size, but generally he was no more than a foot tall, a height he was immensely proud of. According to him he was tall and studly for his kind. And extremely handsome, again, in his opinion. I would grudgingly admit that for his size, he was cute. Maybe if he were five feet taller...

Ree fancied himself a ladies' man, and maybe he was among his own kind. He was always immaculately tailored and groomed, his hair always neatly trimmed. He loved bright colors and dressed accordingly, which was kind of odd for a creature who generally was supposed to remain invisible.

But Ree could sometimes be useful, if you played to his vanity properly, *and* he was in the right mood. I needed his help now. There was no time to waste. The rose was dying on the table before our eyes. I'd have to try harder not to offend him.

It was almost as if he read my mind. He spied the rose and cried out, dropping his spoon with a clatter and coming around the pot of porridge to study it. He made the same two-fingered circle around himself that Maurelle had and muttered some kind of incantation beneath his breath.

For an instant, I swore he paled. I'd never seen him rattled or frightened before. He seldom lost his confident air.

He put his hands on his hips and looked at me with total shocked disbelief. "You went into the forest." He shuddered. "When I cautioned you *specifically* not to. I warned you of the dangers." He shook his head and muttered almost to himself, "How did you get past my defenses?"

This was interesting. Ree *did* care.

"What defenses?" I cocked my head, eager to hear him brag about either the traps he'd set, or the powers he had, powers I didn't already know about. Ready to catalogue them in case I ever needed to get around either of them in the future. "You were sleeping like a baby on the hearth when I left. I walked right past you."

"What?" He physically jumped. "This is bad. Worse than I thought." He shook his head, still so serious that he didn't seem like himself. He was clearly afraid. "You're lucky, Maisie. *Very* lucky to escape the Doove. The Queen of the Unseelie Court doesn't allow trespassers in her forest. If you were so determined to go, you should have taken me with you."

I couldn't tell him in front of Catri that there was no need for the Fear Dorca to bother with me. The Queen had other, much more handsome, prey in her sights. His face swam before me. I swallowed a stab of guilt and worry. What had happened to him? Was he even still alive? Was he being tortured, even as I spoke with Ree?

I shook the vision of his face from my mind and concentrated on Ree. "How could I? You told me not to. You would have tried to stop me."

Ree scowled. "Is that *the* rose?"

Ree lurked everywhere. I had never directly told him my plan, but somehow, he knew anyway. And had apparently tried to stop me. He must have overheard me discussing it with Catri.

"Yes," I said. "It is *the* rose."

He turned up his nose. "It's less impressive than lore would have one think. Not so magical as I imagined." He walked around it, studying it critically. "What are you waiting for? Why haven't you taken it to Maurelle?"

He wasn't, apparently, *as* in the know as I imagined. Then again, he'd been caught napping.

"I tried, but she doesn't want it." Despair washed over me, as unexpected and powerful as fresh grief.

Ree stepped closer and examined the flower closely, inhaling deeply then peering into the bowl where I'd stored the petals. "And no wonder. It's in terrible shape. It's not even sparking. Only weak vibes are coming off it. Like all things that are cut, it's dying. Soon it will have no magic left at all."

"What is he saying?" Catri asked.

"Ree says the rose is dying," I replied.

Catri let out a gasp of horror. "Of course, it is! I wasn't thinking. I should have put it in water right away." Her movements were slow and painful to watch, but I knew her well enough to realize that this was her attempt at quick action.

"Yes!" I pushed my own chair back and sprung to my feet. "I'm clearly too tired to think clearly, too. *Stay*. I'll get it."

"It won't help."

I turned to Ree, surprised by his sympathetic tone.

"Why not?" I asked.

"You don't have the kind of magical water it, or you, need. Even if you did, even magic water can't bring something back from the dead. It could have prolonged the magic a while longer, but we're beyond that now." He touched the rose gently, surprisingly sympathetic and reverent toward it. "It's no surprise Maurelle didn't want it. It takes potent magic to make a beauty potion with any lasting power at all. If the magic is weak, the potion wears off too quickly. To make permanent beauty, beauty of the kind that attracts a king, requires strong magic, indeed."

At least that explained Maurelle's anger and disappointment. To some degree.

Without thinking, I glanced at my hand. How long would *it* stay beautiful?

Ree saw my action and followed my gaze to my beautiful hand. He bounded over and took a closer look. "Too perfect. You've already used it! But I thought it was for Catri. Is that how the rose got in this terrible shape?"

"I *didn't* use it. Not on purpose. The rose *is* for Catri. I'm not sure how my hand got this way. Maybe because I carried the rose with it." I let out a heavy sigh. "That's why we need your help, Ree Ree."

I'd called him Ree Ree when I was small. I hadn't called him the pet name in years. Somehow it had slipped out. "I don't understand *how* this magic works. What can we do? Is there anything we can do with the remains of the rose to help Catri?"

Ree walked back to the rose and circled around it several times, stopping once to peek into the bowl of petals again and stare at them intently. "*Who* did this? This wasn't an accident. This rose was purposefully crushed."

I looked at Catri and shook my head. I had never heard Ree sound or look so serious.

I swallowed hard, not wanting to scare Catri with the details of what happened in the Doove, or how near I'd come to dying at the hands of the Fear Dorca. She was sensitive by nature, and easily frightened and made anxious by even simple things. The aging sickness and its recent rapid progression had made her anxiety worse. I had to shield her.

Ree crooked his finger at me, drawing me close. "*Who?*"

I glanced at Catri and back to Ree. I couldn't say the Fear Dorca's name in front of her. "A darkling. He appeared just after I cut the rose. I didn't even hear him coming. He slapped the rose out of my hand and crushed it beneath his heel before I could stop him."

Catri gasped. The little bit of color drained out of her already pale face. "You faced a darkling?"

I reached over and covered her bony hand with mine. "It's okay. It's over. I'm *fine*."

But Ree wasn't satisfied. "How *did* you escape this darkling?"

"My dagger." I pointed to where it lay on the table. "I lunged for him with my dagger. I barely nicked him. But it was enough. He flew off in a panic, clutching the tiny cut as if I had slashed his throat wide open."

Ree hopped on the pink quartz hilt of the dagger, licked his finger, and touched it to the blade. Then he put his finger in his mouth and sucked. "Iron. You poisoned him, *sorella*."

"What?"

"Iron is poison to darklings, to fae in general, even me. But to a much lesser degree. Smart of you to bring this dagger for protection. Where did you get it?" Ree sounded suspicious. He hopped off the hilt and walked back to the rose.

"It was in Mother's things," I said, feeling the loss of her powerfully. "I only took it because Maurelle told me I needed a sharp knife to cut the rose. It's the sharpest thing we have."

It was also probably one of the most valuable things we owned. Mother had prized it and kept it locked away from us. For our safety, she told us. It was so pretty, like nothing else we owned. With its pink handle, it was a temptation. Its quality was obvious. It had been finely crafted by a skilled bladesmith and was extremely, *exceptionally* sharp.

"Ah. Of course." Ree looked thoughtful. "If a darkling did this, the rose is compromised. Its magic turned dark and unpredictable."

"*What?*" Catri asked. "What is he saying?"

"He says the rose is compromised because of the darkling. Its magic turned dark and unreliable." I glanced at Catri apologetically. "When I told Maurelle about the darkling, she got angry. She told me to bury the rose."

Catri grabbed my hand. "But what about this? What about Maisie's hand?"

Ree's eyes narrowed. "Let me see it."

I sat down again and set my hand on the table in front of him.

Ree walked around it, inspecting it from every angle. "Nice. Very nice magical work." He paused to look up at me. "Did you ask for this? For a new hand?"

"No. Why would I ask for a beautiful hand? I was saving the magic for Catri. I didn't even ask to be healed."

"Wiggle your fingers," he said. "But be careful. Watch out for me."

I rolled my eyes and complied.

"You were gloved when you picked the rose?" he asked.

"No. I held it with my bare left hand as I cut it with the dagger in my right hand."

"With the dagger." He rubbed his chin again, as if that were significant. "When you offered her the rose, Maurelle saw your new hand?"

"No. My hand was gloved."

Ree tapped his chin animatedly, clearly ratcheting up his thinking. "Did the darkling touch the rose with his skin?"

"He may have done," I said. "Not with his heel. He was wearing boots. But at one point, he slapped it out of my hand. He may have done then."

Ree took his time answering. "Then we can't know for sure. But I think you got the good magic before the darkling touched the rose. Or the iron dagger may have poisoned the darkling's dark magic and prevented it from infecting the rose. Impossible to know. They're only theories."

He turned to Catri with a sympathetic look she couldn't see. "Explain the risks and my theories to her. Ask her how much chance she's willing to take in search of a cure. Make clear that, at this point, using the rose is extremely dangerous."

I explained to Catri, gently. "Ree just doesn't know how much, if at all, the darkling corrupted the rose. None of us do. It could cure you. Or kill you. Or do nothing. And anything in between."

"What do *you* think?" Catri looked tortured.

"I think it has to be your choice, and yours alone. I'm so sorry it's come to this." I swallowed my natural tendency to apologize for failing her. There was no need to burden her with my guilt. I didn't want anything to influence her decision.

Catri's gaze fell to her lap and her own bony, heavily veined, age-spotted, arthritic hands. She twisted them in her lap. Finally, she looked up and took my healed hand again, clearly marveling at it.

I squeezed her hand.

"What choice do I have?" she said in a soft, still voice. "The rose won't bloom again for another twenty to thirty years. By then I'll be long gone. At least this gives me a chance. I'll do *anything. Anything.*" She released my hand and grabbed the table for support.

Ree walked over and patted hers with his tiny hand, even though she couldn't see, feel, or hear him. "I make no promises, *sorella*. This could go very badly. Or very well. Or it may not work at all."

He surprised me with his gentleness and sympathy. He'd never called her sister before, either. It was a term of endearment usually reserved only for me, and only used rarely.

"In any case," he continued, "We don't have much time. We must work quickly. Tell Catri to pick up the rose and rub it over her skin, but beware of the thorns. Then draw Catri a bath and boil water for tea."

"Are you actually helping us, Ree?" I shouldn't have voiced my surprise aloud.

"I wouldn't call it helping. I'd call it self-preservation."

I couldn't help smiling. It was like him to deflect.

I blinked back tears. "You've lived in the north too long. You've gone soft and become one of us." I handed Catri the rose and told her the plan, then turned to Ree. "What does tea have to do with it?"

"We're going to make tea from the rosehip." He pointed to it. "It's ripening fast and will soon be rotten if we don't hurry. She'll have to drink the tea hot. With luck, the tea will heal her insides. Then we'll have her bathe in a hot bath of rose petals. We're trying to cover her entire body with the essence of the rose's magic."

CHAPTER 5
THE LAW OF SELECTION

The inkling of hope washed away my exhaustion and quieted the porridge's calls to my empty stomach. I forgot about myself and my own needs as I pulled the tub in front of the fire roaring in the hearth, cut the rosehip from its stem and set it by the fire to dry, handling it with my gloves, and grabbed the kettle and bucket.

Ree followed me outside to the water pump. He jumped onto the faucet. "We must work quickly. Soon the entire province will have heard that you have the rose. Desperate people will do desperate things. Like Catri, many of them won't care that the rose is quite possibly contaminated. They'll come for it. And take it by force, if necessary. As long as any part of the rose is here, we're all in danger."

"I hadn't thought..."

"Of course not. That's why I'm here." Ree tapped his chest. "I'll keep watch, but my protection spell won't last forever. We must use the rose and get rid of it, *publicly*. So there is no doubt we no longer have any bit or petal of it."

"Do you have a plan?" I placed the kettle beneath the spigot and began pumping the handle with force. It felt good to take my frustration out with healthy exercise.

"A plan?" His eyes narrowed. He looked at me like I must be kidding. "I'm *munacielli*. I never plan. That's your job. I act on instinct."

I wasn't so sure I trusted in instinct right now.

Ree cleared his throat. "I didn't want to say in front of your sister." Ree paused and looked out over our small holding, squinting into the distance.

Our chickens pecked in the yard. Our cow chewed the remaining tufts of grass calmly. I didn't see anything out of the ordinary, but Ree was certainly on his guard.

Fortunately, Ree had sharp vision, and a touch of magical vision, as well. "Nothing. All clear." He visibly relaxed, at least a little. "I thought I saw something. False alarm. As I was saying, I didn't want to speak in front of Catri—"

Which was considerate, but funny, really. She couldn't hear him.

"But," he continued. "I've been going to town as often as I can stand it. It's the only way to keep abreast of the news. No small sacrifice. I have to spy on dunces and play up to fools. Your roads are so rough an old man could lose his teeth jouncing across them. Cobblestone—bah!" He made one of his dismissive hand gestures. Ree was a hand-talker. He had a gesture for everything. "No nice warm sewer tunnels or catacombs to travel through, either. So I must face the cold—"

"Yes, Ree. Your point?"

"Rumors, Maisie. The king's men are only a few days away."

"A few days?" I froze with my hand on the pump. "But the journey from the Royal Circle should take weeks. If not a good month, *at least.* Personally, I don't see why the king wants a new bride so badly and so quickly that he would risk the trip with winter fast on our heels. It's a treacherous trip as is in good weather. His last fiancée died tragically in that horrible accident just a month ago. A longer mourning time would surely be appropriate."

"Appropriate, yes. But not in his plans. The official story is that the young king needs a new love to heal his broken heart. I think we both know better than to believe *any* official narrative. The truth is that to be secure on the throne, he needs an heir. For that, he needs a wife."

"True enough," I said. "But he's been through three fiancées now in less than the space of a year. All have died under rather uniquely tragic circumstances before they could be wed. You would think his heart would have toughened up and be hard as stone by now."

I knew what I was saying, though I had to cage my words. One never knew who was listening, even out here in the country. Neighboring house fae could be vicious gossip carriers and they were invisible spies. Ree was protecting against them, but caution had become a habit with me. Everyone suspected the king of being behind the unfortunate selectresses deaths.

"The heart is a fickle organ," Ree said. "But the fact remains—only one more—a girl from this province—stands in his way before he can marry Princess Vahlronia and seal his alliance with her father. They say it's a love match, too. Two viperous beauties in love with their own images—how can they love one another? Maybe it's just power they crave, not passion? We'll eventually see, won't we?"

I used to think Ree could be too cynical. But lately I'd begun to think his cynicism had more merit than I wished.

"If the law didn't require that the reigning king marry a woman from the next province in the sequence established in the constitution after the Great Magic War, he would have married the princess already," Ree continued. "According to the traveler I overheard at the pub a few days ago, a movement to abolish the law has been gaining momentum in the Royal Circle and is spreading through the kingdom. *Rapidly*. 'Like wildfire', were his exact words.

"The palace has been subtly indoctrinating the people, saying the law's outmoded and outdated. Now that so many generations have passed, and the kings have taken queens from all the provinces, the intent of the law has been fulfilled. The goal was always that the ruling monarch would have the blood of the entire kingdom running in his veins, therefore, his allegiance would be to all the people."

"Abolish the law? We've heard nothing." This development filled me with fear.

We had little enough power and representation as it was. If we never even had a shot at having a queen from our province on the throne, where would that leave us? Even now, even as everyone knew our selectress was a sacrifice and would never be queen, we were still afforded honor and power, and a healthy infusion of coin from the king's purse because of the position. At least that had been the case with the provinces of the last three selectresses.

For however long she lived, our selectress would try to influence the king to favor her family and the province. Her family would be set up for life, with more influence with the seat of power than the rest of us would ever have or dream of. The king might even look on us with more indulgence and reduce restrictions here to ease his guilt and make restitution for our loss. That was the hope.

It was why families were so desperate for the beauty the intact rose could have bestowed on some unlucky virgin girl. The more beautiful and beauty-mark-less she was, the longer she would last at court, and the more influence she could build. There was even the naïve hope that the king might fall in love with her and spare her.

But that was wishful thinking in the extreme. Mere justification for sending a daughter to her death. No matter how much the king loved her, he couldn't tolerate a misfit wife. What if she birthed a misfit heir?

"We're too remote and isolated. We're always the last to hear the news," Ree said. "But believe me, the young king would abolish the law. *If* he thought he could get away with it. Lucky for us that the chance of rebellion is still too great. And his armies not strong enough to quell it. *Yet.*"

Better to kill off the innocent women in his way.

I suppressed a shudder. I couldn't think about it. I had enough on my hands with Catri's illness. The law didn't affect us. Neither Catri nor I were beautiful enough to be chosen. Nor did we have enough status, power, or money to make a backdoor deal with the king.

There were girls of privilege in the province whose families had been preparing them since birth for this opportunity, hoping it would arise while they were at their prime. Guarding their virginity as if it were a chest of gold. They would have gladly served an old king, but a young king in need of an heir was much better. The queen who birthed the heir would have more power than any who followed after her death.

These wealthy young women of our province had been tutored and educated in diplomacy and the subtle art of negotiation. They'd been schooled in the ways of the high court, taught manners, and protocol. Taught how to dress and how to flirt while not being vulgar.

Noble families selected the prettiest, and most perfect, of their daughters and did everything in their power to make them even more attractive. It wasn't enough to be pretty. If your beauty mark was too significant, there was no reason for your family to waste time and money priming you for a role you'd never play.

Beauty was now a dual standard, defined in two ways in our province. Before the Royal Circle had become obsessed with *their* version of beauty and perfection, and their ways had subtly migrated north, the lack of an arm or an eye or an ear, having six fingers on a hand, or three legs were all beauty marks of great pride here. And the bigger the obstacle one had to overcome to survive and thrive in our harsh environment, the more respect one was given. It originally meant you, and now meant one of your ancestors, since disfiguring beauty marks were inherited, had served on the frontlines of the Great Magical War. The more severe the mark, the closer to the

front and the source of the magical evil you, or your ancestor, had been.

If you couldn't see or hear or had only one arm to work
your farm or play a musical instrument with, and yet
became a virtuoso, you were highly revered and esteemed.
Our original nobility came from that class of strong people
whose resourcefulness and kind spirits were their true
beauty.

But that had come back to haunt them now. Where
once they had been proud of their unique physicality and
form, after all most people had only two arms and ten toes
in the usual places, for the last several generations, our
lords and noblemen had been marrying the lower classes
and slightly imperfect orphans in an attempt to breed out
the beauty marks. Our province was a repository for the
disfigured and unbeautiful from the other provinces. We
had a shocking number of orphans abandoned on our
figurative doorstep by parents in other provinces who
couldn't stand an imperfection or felt it would bring
dishonor on them.

I was one of those abandoned babies, left on Mother's
doorstep as a newborn. It had always been a puzzle why
my biological mother had abandoned me. I had no beauty
mark. Maybe I simply hadn't been pretty enough for her
tastes, though that theory had problems of its own. It had
been Mother's hope that I would eventually marry one of
our local lesser nobles or well-to-do merchants and
elevate our family out of poverty.

I wasn't beautiful, but I wasn't *bad* looking. My plain
looks and my unknown parentage were strikes against me
landing a high noble. And the suspicion that something

unseen must be wrong with me. Or that I had bad blood. Mothers *never* abandoned their perfectly formed babies here, even if they were exceptionally homely. The other provinces had orphanages for *those* children. It was too much punishment to send one here.

There had never been another baby like me abandoned in all our history. Which made people suspicious. How mentally ill had my biological mother been? How cruel?

But then the idea of my marrying anyone became moot. Catri's aging sickness began accelerating, and then Mother fell ill and died. Now I had Catri to look after. It would be a rare man who would take on both of us. And I wouldn't marry and leave her behind.

Ree grinned sardonically. "Your thoughts are on your face, *sorella*. It was our young king's good luck that the provinces between him and the princess are weak and without the means to do more than demand a farce of an investigation into the deaths of their selectresses. Our province is the weakest of all. Hence the king's desire for speed. And why he doesn't come himself to choose a bride. She's a throwaway, as are we all here."

Ree paused, wearing a pleased expression of one who knows a secret. "But important enough, apparently, to send his younger twin, the prince, in his place."

"The prince is coming?" I hadn't heard, but that explained the recent flurry of activity and Maurelle's desperation for the rose. She was running out of time to find something powerful enough for her rich clients.

"That's the latest rumor," Ree said. "It was decided at

the last minute, apparently. A missive arrived just yesterday.

"We can hope these twins have similar taste in women. Though by all accounts, the two men are quite different."

Ree took a deep breath. "Spring in the Royal Circle is more beautiful than you could imagine, Maisie. What a perfect time for a wedding to the Princess Vahlronia." There was his sardonic humor again.

I focused my anger on the pump handle and began pumping with renewed vigor. "The rumors must be wrong. There's no way the king's men, even with a prince in their party, could get here so quickly. Not unless they flew. The royal dispatch said the king's emissary was leaving only last week. After the war, our people were isolated on purpose, to keep the disfiguring magic and the visible signs of our rebellion from infecting the beautiful people. That's coming back to haunt the king and slow him down." I snorted, taking perverse pleasure in that, at least. "It takes two weeks or more just to skirt the Doove, to say nothing of the rest of the trip."

"They're coming *through* the Doove."

I froze. I gripped the pump handle so tightly that my knuckles turned white. "But the Fairy Queen and her fae? No one gets through her forest."

"Unless they're you—"

"I got lucky."

"Or they have made a deal with the Queen of the Unseelie Court herself for safe passage. Maybe even a treaty or alliance. Why else would the king send his brother?"

The events in the Doove began to make a little more sense. The young man dressed in what was possibly a uniform of the king's army...

"Another reason for us to work quickly and get rid of that rose. The powerful families of the Borderlands have had their time to prepare their daughters cut dramatically in half or less. Their beauty preparations, their negotiations and deals, all under a time constraint now. The young king may make a deal, but he won't suffer an ugly bride no matter how much money one of our nobles throws at him. He can't risk the ridicule.

"The rose is more valuable than ever. I'm still a little surprised at Maurelle's scruples, given what she could have gotten for a potion."

"I'm furious at her." To the point of shaking with anger when I thought about it. "She made me believe that I needed a potion, when all I really needed was the rose. She used me."

"I don't often stand up for witches. But in this, she's right, and honest. A good magic potion would have been better, *sorella*. Even if the rose weren't tainted. A potion can be custom brewed to deliver maximum, lasting healing directed at Catri's specific condition. And gentle healing that doesn't leave hidden scars. It can also be concocted to give ultimate, permanent beauty. Beauty tailored exactly to the king's tastes. A nice side benefit, no? We're playing with fire," he said softly. "Any healing Catri gets could be very painful, and even then, too general to do her much good."

"My hand didn't hurt at all. It was crushed and then it was perfect." I lifted my chin, daring him to contradict me.

"Then you're lucky." He leaned forward with cupped hands to scoop a drink of water.

I set the bucket aside and picked up the kettle to fill.

Ree drank his fill from the drips and shook off his hands, wiping them on his trousers. "Now that I've told you everything I know, it's time for you to be honest with me. What were you *not* saying in there, in front of your sister?"

Ree was too perceptive for his own good, and mine. I hesitated as I positioned the kettle. If I told him that I suspected the darkling was the Fear Dorca, would he try to stop us? And yet...

I swallowed hard. "There was another man in the forest. A young man, very handsome."

The thought that he could have been the prince briefly crossed my mind. I dismissed it. A prince wouldn't have been alone in the forest. A prince wouldn't have risked his life for a peasant girl like me. It was almost ridiculous that even a mere soldier or servant would have.

"Deep in the dark forest and you notice how handsome this young man is?" Ree was clearly trying to put some humor in the situation. "One of the villagers after the rose, too?" But his voice held an edge. He was now thinking what I was and wondering—had I run into one of the king's soldiers?

"No. I didn't recognize him. But he was the darkling's real prey."

Ree stiffened. "The darkling was after *someone*, not the rose?"

"Maybe both. I don't know. I interrupted an abduction." I explained in detail everything I remembered.

As I talked, Ree began pacing up and down the length of the pump. "How was this young man dressed? Is it possible he is one of the king's?"

I shrugged. "Possible, yes. He was dressed in what could have been a uniform of the king's livery. I've never seen the livery in person so it's hard to say."

Ree paled. "The prince?"

I paused, thinking carefully before I answered. I'd never seen the prince, or his likeness. He was rumored to be nearly as handsome as the king. But could one believe rumors?

"I don't think so. He wasn't dressed like a prince. He wasn't even dressed as finely as our earl, even when the earl is dressed for battle. And he certainly didn't *act* like a prince." Though he had been brave.

It was completely beyond my imagination that a prince would save me. Give his freedom, and possibly his life, for mine. I was a person of no consequence.

Ree scowled and muttered beneath his breath, "This could mean war. *Or worse.*"

I ignored his dire muttering. I had more pressing personal matters in mind. "The darkling said the Queen wanted the young man alive."

"That argues for the prince, doesn't it?" Ree was still pale.

"Does it?" I asked, genuinely thinking the situation through. "Or is it more likely that Dark Queen stole a soldier or servant to interrogate to make sure our king is upholding his end of the bargain that you say he made. Maybe to show him that she can snatch his people at will and find out anything she wants at any time. That our king can't hide anything from her. It's a powerful message for her to send."

Ree looked thoughtful. "Maybe so."

I was tired of discussing politics. What good did they do me? I had no power. I could only do my best to protect Catri. "Ree, I think the darkling was the Fear Dorca. I didn't want to say so in front of Catri. From Maurelle's reaction when I described the darkling to her, she believes I'm right. Does that make a difference to the risk of using the rose?"

Ree stopped pacing. "Dark magic is dark magic, *sorella*. The Fear Dorca's is strong, but it doesn't change the situation or the circumstances. Even a small amount will do irreparable damage, whether it's the Fear Dorca's or no." He spoke automatically. It was clear his mind was elsewhere.

We fell silent while I finished filling the kettle, then carried both the bucket and kettle into the house. I set the kettle to boil, dumped the bucket into the tub, and went back to refill it.

CHAPTER 6
CATRI TAKES A CHANCE

Ree supervised the bath and tea preparations with annoying authority and general bossiness.

He hopped onto the table as I prepared the tea.

I reached for the rosehip to crush it and add to the pot of boiling water on the stove.

Ree grabbed my ungloved hand. "No, Maisie! You were doing so well before. Don't touch any part of the rose with your bare skin. Use the gloves at *all* times. We don't want to drain the meager magic that's left."

Catri watched me stop suddenly. "Is Ree talking? What's he saying?"

I explained.

Catri nodded. "Ree's right, Mais. *Listen* to him. The rose has wilted even more since we started making the preparations and drawing the bathwater." Her voice was thin and reedy, with the tremble of an old woman, but I thought I heard an undercurrent of excitement.

As I bent over, Ree leaned in so only I could hear, even though Catri *never* heard him, "And we can't risk further exposure to the potential dark magic to you." He bounded off and dragged a glove across the table to me. For someone so small, he was amazingly quick and strong.

"Yes. Sorry. You're both right. It just slipped my mind." I pulled the gloves on and put the dried rosehip in the mortar, grabbing the pestle. It was going to be awkward working with gloves. "I'm good now, Ree. I can handle it from here. I've made rosehip tea many times."

Ree cocked one eyebrow. "But have you ever made *magical* rosehip tea?"

I sighed as I reached for some dried mint to add a little extra flavor to the tea the way Mother always had. "There's a difference?"

He rolled his eyes. "Shows what you know of magic! Is there a difference?" He made one of his wild gesticulations indicating his frustration with me. "You must add *nothing* to it—no mint. Put that away. No honey. Nothing to sweeten the tea."

Okay, so I didn't know that. I set the mint aside. I would have thought we'd want to sweeten the magic to override any darkness. I apologized to Catri. "Ree says you have to drink the tea plain, without mint or honey. Nothing but rosehip and water."

Catri didn't object.

Ree watched closely, getting in my way, to be honest, as I ground the rosehip and poured it into the boiling water. Then he kept meticulous time, shouting at me to take the pot off the moment he decided it had steeped long enough. "Sieve it! Sieve it now! Into the cup. Make sure there are no rose bits in the cup and don't let any of them drop or touch you. There. *Good*."

I set the steaming cup on the table. "It's time for me to help Catri disrobe and get into the tub. And time for you to disappear and allow her some modesty."

"Yes, yes. But first, we must put the rose petals into the tub."

I picked up the bowl.

"This is important—dump them in all at once. Then give Catri a sip of tea before you help her into the tub. With luck, it will begin healing immediately and help with her stiffness as well as ease her into her magical transformation. She's to drink the rest of the tea while she bathes. She must drink every last drop. And it's critical she get every part of her body wet, even her hair. Anything left untouched will stay unchanged."

My imagination ran wild with images. I shuddered at the thought of the grotesque sight of a beautiful young Catri with one ugly old cheek marring her youthful face. Or her having one withered hand.

I explained to Catri.

"I'm grateful to Ree for his advice and help. Tell him, will you?" she implored.

"He can hear you." I glanced at Ree, who was clearly full of himself, puffed up by the praise. "He looks well enough pleased with himself, believe me."

He grinned. "When you're magnificent, you're magnificent. There's no denying it."

"You can leave now," I said to him.

He shook his finger at me. "Don't dispose of the used tea or bathwater without me. I have to show you how to do it properly. And no soap in the bath. Add nothing. No perfume. No salts. No oils. *Nothing*."

As if we had any of that, other than a cake of home-made soap. "Got it."

"When the water goes cold, get her out. It will do no good for her to sit forever in the cold water except to catch her death." He waited for me to promise before he hopped into the kitchen chair, from there to the floor, and slipped out of the kitchen as if disappearing into thin air.

I forgot all about him as I gave Catri a sip of tea, helped her out of her clothes and into the tub. Lately it hadn't been easy for her to lower herself into the tub. She needed my help to fold her stiff body into the small, low space. But today she slipped in with surprising ease.

Careful not to get any water on myself, I wedged a towel against the back of the metal tub for her to lean against.

She looked up at me. "Did you see that, Mais? Did you see me lower down without groaning? I think it's working. It's working already!"

I wanted it to work as much as she did, but I was trying not to let my hopes fly beyond my control. The despair if they were dashed would be more than I could bear.

"Ree says you have to get every inch of yourself wet, including your hair. But he warned me not to let a drop touch me. The magic must all be for you. Can you get your hair wet?" I handed her a pitcher.

I watched as she moved slowly, but with relative ease compared to her fragile movements lately. When she'd doused herself thoroughly, I handed her the cup of tea. As she soaked in the tub, relaxing in front of the fire, my stomach growled.

Catri had saved me a bowl of cold porridge. Now would be my chance to eat it. But my spoon was missing and the last of the cream was gone. *Ree.*

I found my spoon beneath the cushion of our one good, upholstered chair. Ree just couldn't help himself. But he was being a little obvious, wasn't he? There was no way I'd mislaid the spoon in the chair or that it had somehow dropped beneath the cushion accidentally. *Fine. You're letting me know you're still a house fae from the south.*

As I headed toward the table with my spoon, Catri called to me. "Maisie, could you close the door. It's come open. A cold breeze is coming in."

I rushed to shut it, muttering unflattering things about Ree as I did. He couldn't do something good without ruining his reputation and making up for it by pulling a prank.

Catri soaked in the tub until the water was cold and the tea was gone. It was heartbreaking to watch her stare at her wrinkled hands and body, hoping and hoping, looking for the slightest change. But I was no different. I was watching closely, and nervously, too.

"It's working." She studied her hands. "My age spots look lighter. I *know* they do. And there are fewer of them." She held up her hands for me to see.

"What about my face? Do I look younger to you?" She lengthened her neck and turned her cheek to me, a trick she used to lessen her wrinkles. "Less wrinkled?"

"I think you've been in the water so long that you have prune wrinkles now." I tried to sound light. But the truth was, how honest should I be with her? She looked a *little* younger, I thought. If I squinted. But not young. Not her true age.

"Hand me Mother's mirror. I want to see."

"You can look in the mirror when you're out of the bath. There's no need to rush things."

She paused as if getting up the courage to speak. "How long did it take for your hand to heal? Be honest, Maisie. I need the truth."

"I don't know exactly." Which was the honest truth. "It was still injured in the forest when I put my glove on to carry the rose. I had a hard time getting the glove on over my swollen fingers and palm. And it hurt horribly."

I paused, wondering how much to reveal. "You saw what my hand looked like when I took the glove off here. That's how long it took to heal. The problem is—I have no idea how long it took me to get out of the forest. Time seemed to move differently there. That's my impression, anyway."

"But did you *feel* it healing?"

I shook my head. "I was distracted with fear and survival, and coursing with adrenaline. I was honestly stunned to find my hand like this." I wiggled the fingers of my newly beautiful hand.

Catri hung on my words, clinging onto hope at the same time. "The rose was fresh then, newly cut. More potent. And still it took time. We need to give this time. It has to heal my whole body."

"I agree."

As she nodded, a dark streak appeared in her previously white hair.

I jumped out of my chair. "Catri! Your hair is getting its color back! You have a dark streak." I pointed.

She clapped like a delighted child and grabbed the hair that I'd pointed out. "I *knew* it was working."

"Now that we're sure of it, let's get you out of there." I grabbed a towel and helped her out of the tub, carefully avoiding getting dripped on.

She moved with more ease now. She looked a few decades younger than when she'd gone into the tub. As she toweled off, we both examined her in awe and wonder and utter delight. Her skin was less paper thin and softer. Her veins less prominent. She had fewer age spots and her hair had gone from pure white to gray with streaks of its original dark brown.

I tried to help her dress, but she pushed me away and headed to the cracked full-length mirror on the opposite wall. She preened in front of it, inspecting herself from head to toe. Even peering over her shoulder at her backside.

Her eyes were wide with excitement. "I *feel* better. I *look* better. *Younger.* It's working! It's working, Maisie!" She impulsively hugged me, more tightly than she had in months. "By tonight, I'll be young and beautiful again!" She did a stiff little dance.

I was optimistic, but more cautious. And although she may have forgotten about the potential consequences of using the rose's power, I was still watching for effects of dark magic with a cautious eye.

"You'd better get dressed." I held her undergarments out to her. "Let me help you."

"I don't need help now, Maisie. I'm going to be well. I'm going to be beautiful. *More* beautiful than before. More beautiful *than ever*."

"Let's not get ahead of ourselves." I bit my lip, watching her anxiously. "How are you feeling?"

"Fine. Perfectly fine. Totally lovely." She danced around the room, moving not exactly youthfully, but at least she was moving without pain. "Let's celebrate! Let's break into our stores and bake something luscious and delicious. Let's eat some of the dried berries. Cook them in a pie—"

"Let's not get carried away." But I couldn't help smiling. She hadn't been this energetic in months.

She stuck her tongue out at me, playfully. I hadn't seen her do that in ages, either. It was a girlish gesture in an older mature body, but I was encouraged to see her youthful spirit returning.

She tucked her hair behind her one ear and pulled her hair back from the other side of her head, revealing the misshapen stub of an ear she'd been born with. "Am I growing a second ear yet? Is my one ear beautiful?" She danced to the mirror to look.

Catri's beauty mark since birth had been her stub of an ear. It sometimes affected her hearing, particularly on that side. But it was an easy beauty mark to hide. She simply covered it with her thick hair. We often joked that only having one ear was the reason she couldn't hear Ree. The more severe beauty mark of the aging sickness hadn't appeared until she was eleven or twelve. Poor, Mother. She had blamed herself for it, even though neither she nor Catri's father had suffered from it. So how could they have passed it on? Even so, it had horrified Mother. And her horror of it seemed to go further than her sorrow that her child was sick and would most likely die before her time.

"You just looked a minute ago," I said, humoring Catri. "Can you hear me any better?"

She shrugged.

"There's your answer. You still have one regular looking ear and one stub of an ear. I don't even know what a beautiful ear would look like."

She inspected her ear. "You'd know when you saw it. It will come." As she admired the dark streak in her hair, Ree reappeared, sneaking up on us like always.

His timing was so impeccable, I got the feeling he hadn't been far away. Probably not out of earshot. He put his hands on his hips and studied Catri. "She's looking better. A little younger." He frowned. "She used to admire herself like that when she was small. Before she got sick. I thought she had outgrown it."

"Let her have her fun. Let her enjoy this," I whispered to him. "You'd be admiring yourself, too, if you suddenly looked younger."

He looked at me aghast. "Why would *I* want to look younger? I'm perfect as is. I'm at my prime." He puffed out his chest.

I laughed. He was a vain little creature. But since he'd come from the south, it was hard to blame him for what his culture had trained into him.

Catri spun around. "What are you laughing at? Is Ree back?"

"He is."

"And what does he say about me? Does he notice the difference?"

I hedged, not wanting to add height to her already elevated hopes. "He says you look a little younger—"

"*A little?* I'm decades younger." She shook her finger at open air where she assumed Ree to be, judging from where I'd been looking a moment before. But he'd moved to another spot. "You should learn to flatter and compliment ladies better."

Ree rolled his eyes and bounded over to the cold bath. "I need no lessons. I flatter perfectly but not falsely. Enough of this. We have work to do, Maisie."

Under Ree's instruction, I managed to scoop the rose petals from the bath and set them by the fire to dry alongside the remains of the crushed rosehip. Then I dragged the tub outside and emptied it as far from the croft as I could drag it. Which was much farther than I thought possible. I imagined Ree had something to do with my surprising strength. And I didn't get a drop on myself, either. *Magical.* I usually didn't have much luck not getting soaked by the bathwater.

By the time I finished, the transformation was taking its toll on Catri's energy. Even her excitement couldn't fend off the sudden onset of fatigue.

"Go, get your beauty rest," I teased and sent her to rest in the bedroom she'd shared with Mother on the main floor.

She didn't fight me on it. "When I wake up, I'll be young and beautiful! Anything to help the process along."

While she rested, I did the dishes, then wrapped the stem, dried petals, and crushed rosehips in a scrap of old cheesecloth. All the while I was thinking about what to do with the rose. What was the best plan? Who did I have to fear the most? Who had the most to gain from the rose?

The problem was that *everyone* seemed to have the most to gain. Even if they didn't want the rose for themselves, selling it to the highest bidder would set a poor soul up for life. However, other people had a lot to lose. Like the earl, who was now poised to have his daughter chosen as our selectress. Did that make him more dangerous than the rest? He was certainly the most powerful person in the area. Would I soon find his troops on our doorstep?

Before I'd gone into the forest, none of this had crossed my mind. I'd been blinded with desperation. Single of mind on healing Catri.

In our little village, the earl was the highest ranking noble. We weren't consequential enough to have a duke. The duke lived in the largest town in our province and rarely bothered with us.

The duke had no marriageable daughters. Not even a niece or cousin to offer up. He had a bigger army than the earl. He could crush him in a moment, if he chose. Even if the earl's daughter became selectress, we all knew she would never be queen. Which meant the earl wouldn't be any more of a threat to the duke than he already was.

I had to get rid of the rose in such a way that the earl understood we were no threat to him. And so that everyone else quickly found out that we no longer had it. We needed the earl's protection. But how to get it without endangering Catri's life? My brain was thick with fatigue, only fear and adrenaline were keeping me going. I needed to *think*. But I felt like I was thinking through thick fog.

"Now we implement your plan." Ree rubbed his hands together and looked at me expectantly.

"I thought we implemented *your* instinct?"

"You're the mistress of this house. I'm only the humble servant."

If I hadn't been so tired, I would have laughed. Since when had Ree *ever* been humble? Or a servant? Fatigue was fast catching up with me. I was so tired that I could have fallen asleep on my feet...

I leaned against the table. My head bobbed.

I'm back in the glen, the rose tantalizingly in front of me. Black, odorless smoke curls around me, seemingly rising from the forest floor. But there's no fire, no light producing it. Black wings sparkle menacingly over me. Eyes as dark and fearsome as death stare at me. The mouth of the Fear Dorca curls into a fashion of a smile. "Sleep, little girl, sleep. Let me take you to my queen—"

"Hey, sleeping beauty." Ree clapped sharply in my ear. "Did I wake you? *Sorry*."

I jerked awake, startled, and gasped as if breathing in life. But I'd meant to scream. It had simply frozen in midair.

Ree's face was white and his expression sharp as he watched me. "You're pale as ash and twice as gray. What did you see?"

I took a deep breath and tried to steady my shaking

hands. I didn't want to remember. "The glen. The Fear Dorca. He was coming for me."

Ree looked grim. "Black magic is on the loose. You got too close to the Fear Dorca. No one escapes an encounter with him without consequences."

I wondered how Ree could possibly know such things.

He shook his finger at me. "Fall asleep again before the dark poison in you recedes and you won't wake up again."

He was such a funny, little thing. I tried to ignore his dire prediction and headed for the one good, upholstered chair in our one main room. I just needed to sit a minute and mull through the various ideas I had for getting rid of the rose. Each of them seemed to have a flaw.

Ree beat me to the chair, stationing himself in the middle of the seat cushion where I couldn't avoid sitting on him. "Oh, no you don't. It's not safe for you to sleep yet. We go to town—"

I stifled a yawn. "*No.* We go to see the earl."

My mouth seemed to have decided for me. It engaged before my brain could stop it. Maybe it was protecting me.

"Lord Fanger." Ree studied me with narrowed eyes, but he looked relieved that I wasn't insisting on a nap. "*Why?* You can't possibly trust *him*. I'm surprised you didn't encounter his men in the forest or in the fields between the forest and home. It's an open secret that he wants that rose to protect his daughter's chance at the king."

Ree made a valid enough point. But I had few options.

"I think it better that we should go to town and destroy the rose in the town square, where everyone can see," Ree said.

"I thought of that, but one—will people believe that we've really destroyed the entire thing? And two—destroying it will only anger people who will think I should have given them a chance with the rose, no matter what dangers it poses. Still others will want an explanation of how I came to have it and why I haven't used it for beauty. For myself or Catri. They may even demand to see Catri to make sure I haven't used it. We can't afford that. Not yet.

"And lastly—I don't want to explain about the darkling to a crowd." I shuddered. I was no lover of speaking publicly and had no experience to allay the fear of it. "Who knows how they'll react? Fear drives people to cruelty too often to trust. I don't need a mob to deal with, too."

I took a deep breath to clear my head. "I won't risk running afoul of either the people or the authorities. We still have to live here, after all. We draw enough ridicule and suspicion as it is.

"Let the lord of the region shoulder the responsibility of the rose and any consequences be on him. I'm going to do what any honorable person would do—turn the remains of the potentially dangerous rose over to the most powerful authority in the region."

"He'll use it for his own gain," Ree cautioned.

"Then let him. I don't care. I'll warn him fairly. I've gotten what I wanted from it, as much as can be expected, anyway. Besides, you said yourself that the rose has little to no magic left. What harm can it really do?"

"Hmm." Ree appeared to mull over my plan while he

sat comfortably in my chair. "What about getting the word out?"

"You needn't worry about that. As soon as his servants see I've come for an audience with him, and what I've brought, word will spread. Like Mother always said, servants and tradesmen are notorious gossips. If you want to spread a rumor, start with them. If I'm lucky, the good lord himself will even send out a proclamation."

"Lord Fanger's only daughter is generally considered the most beautiful, least beauty marked girl of the province. The villagers are placing bets that she'll be the king's emissary's choice. She has the right pedigree, too. But then you know that, *sorella*."

I smiled slyly. "Very perceptive, Ree. Lady Brinley is very beautiful and her beauty mark barely noticeable. She has no pressing need of the rose. But my giving it to her father anyway, should keep us in the lord's good graces. He has the power to destroy the rose's remains without public censure or fear of reprisal. He's surely smart enough, cautious enough, even ruthless enough, not to risk using any remaining trace of dark magic on his beloved daughter, his hope for more glory and power. He might even be grateful that the rose won't be able to produce competition for her and reward us accordingly."

Ree's eyes sparkled. "You're a wily one, my Maisie. I have taught you well."

"You've taught me?" I looked at him in amazement. "*I* thought up the plan."

"Yes, but *I* made you think on it." He tapped his chest.

"I'll get my cloak." There was no use arguing with him. But I hesitated in front of the peg that held my cloak.

"What about Catri?" I bit my lip. "It's not wise to take her with us just yet. It's not likely, unfortunately, but if she suddenly transforms into a beauty rivalling Lady Brinley..."

"Yes, yes, *sorella*. That's the way to think. She stays here and barricades herself in. It's important that no one sees yet that the rose has helped her. That will only make a thief more determined. Until everyone knows that we no longer have the rose, she's not safe."

She may not be safe even then, I thought, grimly. I had to convince the earl she was no threat.

"Tell her not to open the door for anyone." Ree began gesticulating wildly, like he did when he was excited. "Not even if they sound and look like us."

"You mean like *me*. She can't see *you*."

"Whatever. She must stay out of sight and be brave."

"If the house is barricaded, how will we get back in?" I asked, logically enough.

"Leave that to me."

I sighed. Ree wasn't the most reliable, but he'd proven trustworthy enough these past hours. I had no other choice.

I heard Catri stirring in her bedroom. I tapped gently on her door and slipped inside to relate the plan and pass along Ree's instructions and strict warning to her.

"Not even to you?" she asked, as I had.

"To no one. He's afraid someone might impersonate us and harm you even though you no longer have the rose." I was thinking of a witch or a fae in the employ of a human who wanted the rose.

"You have magic on the brain." Ree had somehow

76

silently followed me in and listened in. "But also, I fear someone may try to take us hostage and use us to gain access to the cottage."

"That's reassuring," I whispered to him, wishing he weren't always so frank. "But we'll have what's left of the rose on us. If it comes to that, we'll hand it over."

Ree shook his head. "Will we? What if they take us when we're on our way home, after having visited the earl? We'll be emptyhanded then. Will they believe us?" He waited for me to praise his thinking.

I bit my lip. "We'll ask for a receipt from the earl. That will be our proof to anyone who questions us. We'll get his seal. No one will doubt that."

Ree shook his head. "I'm not convinced of this plan. We can't risk dark magic falling into the wrong hands, even if the chance of it is remote. Can we trust the earl to not let that happen?"

"No one would dare go against the earl."

"You think too small, *sorella*. No human, maybe. But believe me, even though Maurelle is afraid of the rose, there are others much more powerful than her who will want it precisely *because* it may contain dark magic. We must convince the earl to destroy the rose for us."

I went cold. "I have no influence over an earl. As I said, let the consequences be on him. Destroying the rose is in his best interest."

Catri sat up in bed. "Is Ree in the room? Tell him it's not polite to visit a lady's bedchamber without her invitation." She laughed. She had carried Mother's hand mirror into bed with it. She picked it up and took another look at herself, and with a smile that should have warmed my heart, crossed her heart. "Go. Go to the earl. I won't let anyone in. I promise. No one, Mais. Least of all *you*." She laughed.

But I looked out her bedroom window at the Doove and shuddered. I could feel it watching us.

CHAPTER 7
TO LORD FANGER'S CASTLE

I would have preferred to be travelling with a legion of soldiers for protection. Instead, I had Ree and Mother's iron dagger. It was late afternoon already. We had to make haste. This far north this time of year, the days were short.

I half expected rain and gloom to descend upon us. To drench us in our quest for safety and order. But the afternoon remained surprisingly clear still. With the swirl of evil that I could feel in the forest at my back, and the sense of impending ambush around us, it seemed only fitting the weather should match the mood. More practically, the weather here was completely changeable from one minute to the next. Sun then rain, then even snow. But it remained one of those beautiful fall days that made my heart ache with missing Mother and long for things I couldn't name.

The low angle of the sun made colors vibrant and the shadows long. Golden hour would soon be upon us, when the light was truly magical, flattering the scenery to show its most magnificent beauty.

Ordinarily, I loved this time of day. But since coming out of the Doove, shadows felt like my enemy. Even worse, Ree insisted we stay in them, lurking like dark fae among them. Keeping out of sight.

I had to hand it to Ree—he knew his way among the shadows. He knew how to stay invisible, though I was less skilled. Short an army of bodyguards, this was our best option.

Although we walked away from the Doove toward town, I could feel the Doove at my back. And the face of the young man in the forest wouldn't leave me alone. When I closed my eyes or let my mind wander, he appeared in my thoughts.

Prince? No, ridiculous.

I couldn't come to grips with my reaction to him—guilt, worry, and admiration. Longing, maybe. His beauty had been magnificent, even bruised and beaten. But his heart...

I swallowed hard, feeling as if I'd betrayed him. And yet, I'd done as he'd asked. I'd given him the gift of saving me. I hoped it was gift enough for him wherever the fae had taken him.

Staying in the shadows of this open, rocky, barren land of ours was no easy task. Aside from the Doove, the land was mostly scrubby fields and rocky outcroppings. Tall hills and small mountains of nothing but rock where no trees grew, only moss and lichen.

The landscape was dotted with clumps of bushes and the odd bunch of trees. A small white house or cottage here and there, which we avoided. Rocky fields covered with tufts of wild grass, much of it now golden tipped with autumn. Occasionally, a brook or stream with rocky shores and the odd scraggly tree growing on the bank. Everything here was rocky.

Outsiders would describe the scenery as dramatically beautiful or rugged. And that it was. But it was no good for hiding. Or for producing valuable crops.

The wealth of our province, if you could call our meager earnings wealth, was mostly in peat and the fine whisky our unique peat and water flavored. Even that much prosperity, discovered on the backs of the generations of our ancestors who were banished here, was begrudged us by the South and particularly the Royal Circle. Though they bought our spirits in large quantities, they taxed it heavily and handed out licenses even more sparingly. The earl, of course, had the most profitable whisky license in our village and surrounding territory. In all of the province, only the duke had a better license, mostly because he had better peat and more power.

The road into the village was little more than a muddy trail this time of year. Soon it would be a snow-covered path. Even so, in an abundance of caution, we skirted it.

Ree was much quicker and more agile than I was. He bounded here and there and could hide in a clump of grass if he chose. Following him, keeping up with him, was a challenge.

Fortunately, the earl's castle sat on a promontory that spanned out into the only lake of our territory. The lake was fed by a stream that came through the Doove. Some said it was forest magic that made the water so good and tasty for whisky. That there was a touch of fae magic in it. Dark fae's magic or light fae's? That was the eternal debate.

People argued either side of the question. The whisky certainly could be used to numb blinding pain. And with the pain relieved, miraculous healing often followed. It was a mercy, too, to be able to give it to the critically ill and dying and ease their way out so they left this world peacefully.

On the other hand, maybe dark fae magic explained the whisky's strength and the visions and hallucinations it occasionally produced in those who became drunk on it. The hallucinations, however, could be pleasant or terrifying. And there seemed to be no reason to who got what kind of hallucination. Some men got drunk and beat their wives and children. Others became mellow and thoughtful, transformed from earlier violence. But many a good man had become drunk and thought he could fly, then jumped to his death from one of our rocky peaks. But it was those very qualities, and the apparent thrill of the roll of the dice, that made our whisky in such demand in the South.

Local myth held that our late queen, mother of the current young king, had bathed in the waters deep on the other side of the Doove in an effort to seduce the Fairy King of the Seelie Court. She had hopes of conceiving a male heir, one with extreme power, that would rival the fae and be able to conquer their kingdoms. The first five queens of the late king had either been unable to give him an heir or had produced only sickly male babies that died before their first year. The king was getting old and had no issue.

How the queen could possibly pass off a bastard as the king's son surely put this plan in peril. But the fact was that the young queen gave birth to twin boys not eight months after her wedding. Twins being born a month early was not so surprising. Twins rarely went full term. The earliness of the boys' births weighed neither for nor against the theory.

Their mother lost her life giving birth to them, but the boys were strong and healthy. Surprisingly, the old king mourned her and never married again. But he was well pleased with the boys she'd produced and claimed them as his own and his heirs. Both of them looked just enough like the king that he couldn't be ruled out as their sire. But, then, the queen had been a not so distant relative of his, which could explain the resemblance, too.

One of those boys was now the young king, and the other, the younger, his twin brother, was supposed to be among the emissary party the king was sending to find him a bride. The party that was coming through the Doove with haste.

Ree peeked around a bend in the road that hugged the hill it was carved into. He held me back with his hand. Then, deciding the way was clear, beckoned me on.

The castle was surrounded on its peninsula by stone walls made from local stone. It was strategically placed to be able to protect the lake and watch in all directions for invaders. It had the extra protection of being an island at times, too. Particularly when the Doove fed the lake in the early spring. At those times, if the drawbridge that spanned to the shore was up, it was accessible only by boat.

Our summer and early fall had been dry. The lake was largely mud flats now with sludgy, stale water sitting in pools here and there. The earl would be praying for rain to fill the lake for his whisky. Even so, I enjoyed the sight. The lichen and moss covering the flats and exposed rock were golden with fall and beautiful to my eye.

Ree and I were able to pick our way across the mud flats to the big stone bridge. I tried not to gawk too much as we crossed it, hurrying along as fast and inconspicuously as possible.

I had eyed the gray fortress from shore my entire life, shuddering at its foreboding presence when I should have taken comfort from its strength perhaps. It was supposed to be there to protect us, the people. But fantasy and ideals rarely meet reality. In truth, the castle represented our elite and authority. Neither had treated my family well. I had no reason to either love or trust them.

For all that gawking of my youth, I had never been to the castle proper. Never set foot on the cobblestone surface of the bridge. I found it imposing. My heart raced. I had to force one foot in front of another. I hoped I had the courage to do what must be done.

I had only seen the earl once or twice in town, but he had never taken any notice of me. And why should he? I was too far below his station, just a poor, strange, plain girl from an outcast family. Our only hope of getting an audience with him now was that he kept abreast of local news and gossip as a way of maintaining his power. I was betting that he had already been informed that I had the rose. Had maybe even paid spies for the information. He had them everywhere.

It was the earl, and his men, that I feared most of anyone mortal. Feared that they would come to our cottage and lock Catri away in some dank dungeon until she either died or it was clear she was no threat to the earl's daughter and power. Catri, though, had seemed unaware of that danger. What good would health, or even beauty, do her if she died imprisoned in a dank dungeon?

I had to play this situation carefully. But did I have the wit and guile to do it properly, not to mention the nerve?

Tried by fire. That's what Mother always said brought out the steel and the worth of a person.

All visitors to the castle had to go through the castle gate and were only allowed inside the walls with the earl's express permission. Tradesmen and laborers went in and out without much trouble. But people like us? Like me, really, because only I could see Ree.

Ree, of course, was unconstrained by such a barrier, and made a point of showing off by slipping inside past the bars and making faces at the guards, who couldn't see him. He danced on the green lawn just on the other side and made eyes at pretty maids walking the grounds.

I was forced to step out of the shadows and announce myself to the guard, who looked me over with obvious disdain. With my wild hair, my muddy skirts, and the dark circles beneath my eyes from exhaustion, even without a mirror, I was certain that I did *not* make anything near a pretty picture. Nor did I look like gentry.

"State your business," the guard said, unnecessarily gruffly, I thought.

I lifted my chin and balled my gloved hands into tight fists, hoping he wouldn't search me and find the dagger I carried for protection tucked into my skirts. "I'm here to see the earl."

"He's expecting you, is he, lass?" His tone was nearly a sneer. He was mocking me. His gaze travelled lewdly over me, passing over the dagger. "What could *you* possibly have to offer that the laird would want?"

I steeled myself, praying that my voice wouldn't tremble. "A magic rose. Is that sufficient?"

The guard stared at me, practically slack jawed. Maybe my outward confidence had stunned him. Or maybe he'd heard about the rose by now, too.

"Tell him that Maisie Jayne Rose requests an immediate audience to discuss the Doove rose."

The guard's eyes narrowed. For a second, I thought he would turn me away. Instead, he made a sound deep in his throat and barked an order to someone inside the gates. He returned his attention to me. "Wait where you are. We'll see what the earl says." He didn't sound optimistic on my behalf.

While we waited, Ree amused himself by running around the lawn and courtyard, causing as many minor annoyances for the guards and laborers as he could get away with. Knocking over a pile of horseshoes the blacksmith was working on and causing a clatter. Startling a knight's horse that was being exercised in the yard. Smothering the fire that was going in the courtyard until it merely sputtered. And hiding the washerwomen's clothespins.

I shook my head at Ree, warning him to stop. But he

was having too much fun. I mouthed to him, *They're going to think I'm bad luck. They'll never let me in then.*

Ree sulked, but he restrained himself. *Some.*

Finally, a runner came back and whispered in the guard's ear. The guard turned to me. "The earl will see you. He's a busy man. Busier than usual with the prince coming. You'd better not be wasting his time." He opened the gate begrudgingly.

I smiled darkly at him, telling him with my body language that because I had the rose, I had power. He'd best not mess with me. It was all false bravado.

"Follow him." The guard nodded toward the runner. "He'll take you to the castle."

I walked through gate, feeling the odd combination of relief at being under the earl's temporary protection and a pang of fear at becoming his prisoner. Or leading my sister to the slaughter.

The gate clanged closed behind me, reminding me that I would have to play this situation carefully. A gate wouldn't stop the fae, but at least it would stop any mortals who were currently stalking me. But would that be any comfort if I had just walked into the lion's den?

I motioned to Ree to follow us and hurried after the runner through the courtyard, which bustled with activity. Getting ready for the prince's arrival, I surmised. A king's visit, even a king's emissary's visit in the form of a prince and his party, was an honor and a great expense.

The castle windows were being cleaned and a mason was busy making minor repairs to the castle's gray, stone masonry. The blacksmith was busy making new shoes for the horses. The tanner was polishing saddles. A variety of merchants and farmers were arriving with goods and foods of all kinds. The bustle was impressive in its scope and the sight of all that good food made my mouth water. When had I ever tasted bread as fine as I saw being brought into the castle?

Chickens strutted around the yard. A servant came out and tossed them crusts of stale bread. *Even the chickens feast better than I do.*

The castle was a village in miniature unto itself. Most of these tradesmen lived in the village and came in to work for the day. But some of them lived within the castle walls, as well.

The runner ignored them all and led me across the courtyard, past a raised bed of bright fall foliage, up a set of stairs and into the impressive great hall of the castle.

"Wait here."

He didn't offer me a seat, nor a drink of water and certainly not a cup of tea. Of course, he didn't offer Ree anything—he couldn't see him. And he would never have stooped to offering hospitality to a house fae even if he could see him.

I stood awkwardly, trying not to gawk at the great hall around us. It was a man's hall, a warrior's tribute, and a museum to war all at the same time.

An elaborate tapestry depicting the deciding battle from the Great Magic War nearly covered one wall. The earl's ancestor was at the forefront, charging into battle.

It would be treason to have such a thing in the Royal Circle, or for any of us to display, as well. The battle was depicted too accurately and not to the official narrative of the ruling class. Even I could see that. The earl must be very powerful, indeed, to display it so casually. More powerful than I imagined.

On another wall hung a painting of the first earl looking fierce and uncompromising in his battle gear. The first of his line to be beauty marked, his long six-fingered hands were gloved in fine leather and showed off prominently by the artist. The current earl had only one six-fingered hand, or so I'd been told. The curse—I didn't like that word—was either waning or being bred out. A portrait artist today would certainly hide, rather than feature, the current earl's beauty mark.

The rest of the three-story hall was decorated with weaponry of all sorts and from many time periods—bows and arrows, spears, swords, and battle axes. Even tattered flags. They were arranged in artistic circles, half circles, and quarter circles as they hung on the walls. A statue of the first earl mounted on his mythically brave horse sat on the ornately carved mantle of a large fireplace where a tame blaze flickered.

Servants came and went as we waited, ignoring us. I worried as the time passed that we would be sent away, out into the twilight, or worse, darkness, to find our way home. And that was the better of the scenarios running through my too active mind.

The earl's captain of the guard burst in and strode through the hall with a fierce expression, ignoring the bustle. Something was up. Something was wrong. My ears perked up. The time was ripe for listening.

I motioned to Ree and whispered beneath my breath, taking care not to move my lips, "See what you can find out."

Ree didn't need my urging. He'd already sensed the same. He took off, darting here and there to avoid being underfoot, until he disappeared down a corridor.

I was left to stand alone with my thoughts, hoping Ree would return soon.

CHAPTER 8
A DEAL FOR THE ROSE

While I waited at the earl's pleasure, I watched the constant bustle as servants polished the room around me. A dressmaker and her assistants arrived with great piles of expensive fabrics. For Lady Brinley?

As if I'd conjured her myself, Lady Brinley came into the great hall from an adjacent corridor, laughing and surrounded by a group of servants and ladies of her acquaintance.

Lady Brinley barely noticed the commotion around her. To ignore the work being done on your behalf was the privilege of wealth.

I slunk closer to the wall, preferring to be invisible. But for some reason, her gaze swung my way and our eyes met. For just an instant, I saw the small girl she'd been and remembered the easy friendship we'd had as we'd played on the edge of the forest while her mother, the countess, bargained with my mother for something or other I couldn't remember. Or maybe I'd never known. But they'd come regularly. For a while. Until the earl found out, I imagined now.

It hadn't seemed so improbable then to the child that I was that an earl's daughter would be out running errands with her mother, the countess. Or that they'd want something from my mother. Or that the earl's daughter would be allowed to play with Catri and me. But now it struck me as very odd. I wished I could step back in time and ask Mother what that was all about.

Sadly, the clearest memory was of the earl's men showing up and dragging both the countess and her daughter away. And calling me an ugly bastard child.

I'd caught glimpses of Lady Brinley only rarely since then. The earl kept her well hidden inside his fortress. She had grown very lovely. Her hands were folded demurely in front of her, revealing her beauty mark. But you had to know to look for it. Unlike her six-fingered father, who used his extra finger expertly and to his advantage, Lady Brinley had the merest little stump of an extra finger so fine as to be almost invisible.

No wonder the earl had such high hopes for her.

Our gazes held for no more than an instant. But her eyes registered recognition and shock. And something else. Maybe guilt or embarrassment. She quickly averted her gaze. And when she swept past me, she didn't acknowledge me.

After that, time dragged. I was eager to be done with my business with the earl and back on the road before it got dark. Eager for Ree to reappear. Hoping that I would be allowed to leave, and that the earl wouldn't arrest

Catri. That he hadn't already sent a contingency of his men to take her into custody.

I couldn't tell how much time passed, but I was finally summoned by a brusque servant and told to follow him. He led me down a different corridor than Ree had disappeared down. I was nearly knocked aside as the earl's captain of the guard burst by, his face tight with anger.

The servant stopped before a door. He rapped lightly, then pushed the door open. "Miss Maisie Jayne Rose, my lord."

I peeked past the servant. The earl sat behind an enormous carved wooden desk, seated before a sumptuous bookcase filled with leather books. A fire blazed on the wall to his right. The room was comfortably warm and could easily make me sleepy and dull. He was busily writing some kind of missive, his face tight with tension.

"Send her in." He didn't bother to look up.

The servant stepped aside to let me pass. I took a few tentative steps into the room, just enough so that the door could close behind me. As the door swished closed, Ree darted in.

I could have collapsed with relief. I hadn't realized how attached I was to Ree or how much I was counting on him to be with me. And create a distraction if it were necessary. Though I couldn't see myself escaping no matter how large a disruption Ree caused in the earl's office. At the same time, I wanted to chide Ree about cutting things so close, but I couldn't risk either giving his presence away to the earl or looking like a crazy person talking to air. Not everyone believed in house fae.

"I said come in, didn't I? Come closer. I don't bite." The

earl waved me closer, still not looking up. Finally, he signed whatever he was writing with a flourish, set down his pen, folded the letter and sealed it with wax and the seal of his signet ring. At last, he looked up to where I stood trying not to cower or lose my nerve in front of his desk.

His eyes narrowed as he looked at me. "What's this about a rose?" He sounded curious enough, but too inno‑cent. I was certain he'd been fully briefed already. And more than likely furious that the soldiers he'd sent out after the rose had failed.

"Not just *a* rose, my lord. The *Doove* rose." I pulled the cheesecloth wrapped parcel and set it in front of him on the desk.

He looked at it almost incuriously, but his eyes glit‑tered. I wondered whether it had been a mistake to toss the rose out before him so boldly. Maybe it would have been better to hold it in reserve. But what was the point of that? I didn't need his guards pawing me and feeling me up as they searched my person for it.

"Why are you wearing gloves?" the earl asked. "Is it so cold in here?"

Did he think I was insulting his wealth and status? Or did he fear I was hiding an extra finger? The earl had enough bastards in the territory. Could he think he'd sired me?

"No, my lord. I wear them so as not to touch the rose with my bare hands."

"Unless my eyes deceive me, it's already covered in cheesecloth. Is it so dangerous?"

"It *may* be, my lord." I let my words dangle in the air,

as if I were underplaying the rose's power and danger intentionally. I cast my eyes downward, trying to look humble, but, really, I was furiously thinking. "It would take someone more experienced with magic, and more learned, than myself to say for sure."

I didn't care whether he thought me ignorant or not. It was better for me if he *did* underestimate me.

"If you're here to try to sell me a worthless flower, you've wasted both our time. Roses are common enough."

I raised my gaze and one eyebrow. "This time of year, my lord?" I spoke softly, keeping my rising anger alive just enough to cover my fear.

He was playing a game with me as if I were a mouse. But he was mistaken—I wasn't a mouse. I worried anew that he had already sent guards to retrieve Catri and bring her to be imprisoned here in his dungeon. That he was only trying to get as much information as possible from me.

"Have you seen any other roses, blooming then, my lord? If you have, I must compliment the garden." I tried to look demure.

He sneered. "*That* doesn't appear to be a rose at all."

"Not a whole rose. But it looks very much like what it is, a dissected rose. You can see through the cloth that it's fresh enough. And to answer your original question—I'm not here to sell you *anything*."

I paused for drama. "I'm here doing my duty as your loyal citizen. I'm here to turn the rose in to you as the ultimate authority of the territory. Even the remains of the Doove rose are far too dangerous to leave lying around. You, my lord, with your power and wisdom will know what to do with it." My words seemed to surprise him.

He stroked his mustache, though I don't think I'd managed to stroke his ego as much as hoped. "I've heard the gossip. It's true then, you succeeded. The witch, Maurelle, was very keen to have the rose. She sent half the territory out after it."

Including his own men, but he didn't seem to want to admit that to me.

"Now she claims it's tainted and won't get near it," he continued. "Do I have my facts right?"

I nodded. "It *may* be tainted, yes."

"You don't know?" He was trying to be clever, but he was clearly prying for more information. I was sure stories were already circulating.

"A darkling may or may not have touched it. It's hard to say for sure." I refused to cower.

He studied me as if trying to figure out how a slip of young woman had retrieved the rose and out maneuvered his much braver, stronger, well-armed, well-trained men.

He gave me a little wave of his hand, his six fingers rippling. "Explain."

Ree explored the room while I carefully told the earl as little as I could while appearing to tell the whole story. I again omitted the part about the young man the Fear Dorca attacked. Something kept cautioning me not to mention him.

"So you can't be certain the Fear Dorca *did* touch it?" The earl rubbed his lip. Avarice lit his eyes.

"No, my lord. I can't."

His gaze ran up and down me. "It doesn't appear that *you've* used the rose."

If he meant to cut me, he fell short. I wasn't consumed with being beautiful. Like power, beauty brought its own troubles.

"No. As you can plainly see, I have not. It's far too dangerous. I'm not a risk taker." I swallowed hard.

The entire journey here, I'd been weighing whether to admit that Catri had or not. What was the safest course for all of us? Sooner or later, though, people were bound to see her or guess.

His eyes lit up.

"But my sister has."

The light left his eyes. His expression became hard. "I thought you just said it was too dangerous."

"I did. And it is—for someone in full health. You may not be aware, but my sister is dying of the aging sickness. Which was why I risked my life going into the Doove for the rose. Without a cure, she'll die soon. A few more months at most. She made the choice herself to try the magic. If the dark magic had killed her, or kills her still, she'll be no more dead than from the disease."

Lord Fanger's eyes flashed. "And is she? Beautiful, I mean?"

Of course, that *was* top of his mind, not Catri's restored health. Which told me everything I needed to know. If Catri were beautiful, she was a threat. And the rose was something he wanted desperately.

I took a deep breath, relieved for the moment to tell the full truth. "No."

He had a hard time hiding his pleasure. He was good

with masking his thoughts, but I was equally good at seeing past the mask.

"The rose didn't work? Then why bring it to me and waste my time?"

"I didn't say it didn't work *at all*. Catri's not beautiful, and she's not young again. Not her true age, surely. But she has a dark streak in her hair now amongst the pure gray that had been there before. And she can move more easily and without pain than she could a day ago. She looks maybe ten or twenty years younger. Which sounds like a lot until you realize she looked eighty or ninety before and she's less than twenty in reality."

"Where is this sister of yours? Why haven't you brought her with you, to prove it? I'd like to see this magic with my own eyes."

I had to weigh my words carefully. "What good would that do, if you hadn't seen her just before? How could you judge? She's still frail and very tired. Do you expect a sixty or seventy-year-old woman to walk all the way here?"

His eyes narrowed. I'd been too impertinent. But he was restrained by the hope that I would give him still more information.

"You're free to send one of your servants to check on her and report back. Or send someone from the village who's seen her recently." There would be few to none of those. "Or come yourself. The lord of the realm is always welcome at our humble abode." As if he would.

"I can have her brought to me."

I didn't respond.

He continued scrutinizing me. Maybe he wasn't used

to honesty. *Pity.* "What do you expect me to do with this?" He pointed to the cheesecloth package on his desk.

"I don't have your maturity and wisdom, my lord. If it were me, I might destroy it. Alas, I have no idea how to do that safely. Or in a way that will convince the village that it's been done." I paused, staring at him unblinking.

Maurelle had told me to bury it. But what was the sense of that if someone could find it and dig it up?

"I believe its magic is weak, if not extinct. Otherwise, it would have cured Catri completely and made her beautiful beyond all imagination. The rose no longer glitters as it did when I first picked it."

Ree had climbed up on a stack of books on one of the highest shelves behind the earl. He had his back braced, poised to knock the stack over on the earl if he had to. He made a slitting motion across his throat. Apparently, he thought I misspoke.

I ignored him. "By the time I got out of the forest, the rose was already in very bad shape. It's wilted more since. I made tea out of it for Catri. The dried remains of it are there, as well as the remains of the stem and the petals and leaves."

"That's all of it? Every piece?" the earl asked.

"I hope so. Petals were falling off as I ran out of the forest. I tried to get them all. I *think* I was successful. But I can't be sure. One may have escaped me without my notice. It was black dark in the woods." I suppressed a shudder at the memory. "That's everything I have, or ever *have* had, of the rose."

Lord Fanger considered me. "You've heard that I've offered a reward for the rose?"

I hadn't heard. I really hadn't. I'd been too preoccupied with Catri to listen outside our world or pay any attention. But it didn't surprise me.

He rang a bell and a servant immediately appeared. He motioned with his two forefingers for the servant to come forward. "My purse."

The servant had anticipated his master. He pulled a small purse from his belt and handed it over, then left the room.

Lord Fanger pulled out a gold sovereign and set it on the desk between us. "Your reward."

Did he think I'd sell so cheaply? What kind of a fool did he take me for?

"I don't want your coin."

"What I fairly offered, you should take." He pushed the money closer.

I held my ground, silent.

He pushed his chair back and went to a cupboard. He returned with a small bottle of his best whisky, a medicinal size. "For your sister's good health."

I met his gaze. Catri was my weak spot. I wanted the lovely whisky in case the aging sickness returned. I swallowed hard. We still wouldn't be safe, not as long as he, or anyone, feared that Catri would become a beauty before the prince chose his brother's bride. "In addition to what you offer, I want a ride home. And several of your guards to remain with us and protect us until after the prince and his party have left.

"In return, I promise that neither Catri, nor I, will seek the king's hand. No matter how beautiful Catri becomes, which I don't expect. Neither of us want to be queen. We'll stay in our cottage, far from sight. Your guards will be with us to make sure we keep our word and to protect us from anyone who still thinks we have the rose."

"Done." He shoved the coin and the whisky at me.

"I relinquish all rights to the rose to you." I reached for the coin, relieved that I'd bargained out of him imprisoning us here.

He sprang forward from his chair and gripped my wrist so tightly it throbbed, his six fingers pressing into my skin. "How did a slip of a girl like you defeat the great darkling? What aren't you telling me?"

From high on his shelf, Ree leaned against the stack of books, pushing them toward the edge. But before he could accomplish it, the fire gave a great roar and a pop. An ember the size of my palm bounced out if the grate onto the carpet and hissed.

The earl released my wrist and ran to tamp it out before it caught the entire beautiful carpet on fire. Or burned down the castle.

My wrist throbbed as I rubbed it gently, watching in horror. "I told you *everything*, my lord. I used the iron dagger. You have dozens of similar daggers hanging on your walls."

He looked over his shoulder at me with gleaming eyes as the ember finally died out beneath his boot. He glared at *me* as if *I* were a witch. As if the darkling had imbued *me* with darkness. "Larkus! Larkus. Where is that cursed butler?"

I had no defense. I hadn't encouraged the fire. Ree, my protector, was staring down at us with his back still to the books, straining and shoving with a pink face.

Larkus appeared, quickly taking in the scene. "I'll take care of the carpet, my lord—"

Just at that moment, Ree managed to topple the books. They fell from the shelf, fluttering like butterflies. One solidly hit the chair where the earl had been sitting moments before. One bounced off it. The remaining volumes flapped to the floor directly.

Lord Fanger scowled and strode back to his desk with his face full of fury. He grabbed the gold coin and the whisky and thrust them into my hands. "Take your coin and be out of my sight."

"My guards?"

"Yes, yes. You can wait for them in the great hall. Larkus, send for the captain. I have instructions for him." He dismissed me with a wave of his hand.

Ree bounced down the bookcase and followed us out. "Did you see that? A *direct* hit." He was as pleased with himself as if he'd slayed a dragon. "I have your back, *sorella*. There is no doubt. If that fire hadn't interceded..."

CHAPTER 9
CATRI DESPAIRS

By the time we arrived home, it was dark. The senior guard of the small group the earl had dispatched with us helped me down off the wagon. The others stationed themselves outside our door and around our small property.

I hated to admit it, but I was glad for their presence. Glad for the ride home in their cart. Glad we didn't have to traverse the darkness ourselves. Glad my plan had worked. *For the moment.*

Ree bragged all the way home. But I got the feeling it was more to cover the feeling of tenuous safety he must have felt as keenly as I did. Our fragile safety was balanced by our precarious position.

I just hoped the guards didn't slit our throats in the night or burn us to death in our cottage. I had the earl's word, and I had the suspicion that he wanted to keep an eye on me for a while to see if I was conjuring magic. And to see how much the rose magic worked on Catri and whether there were any ill effects. But when he was done with us? Would he keep his bargain then?

The senior guard walked me to the front door. I hesitated and looked to Ree for help. How were we to get in? He'd already disappeared.

The guard looked at me like I should let us in.

"I told my sister to barricade herself in while I was gone. Give her a moment to realize we're here and let us in." I wrapped gently on the door. "Catri? Catri, *it's me.*"

If she obeyed our instructions, she wouldn't let us in.

But the door swung open. Ree stood inside the cottage, grinning as he let us in. Catri sat at the table, slumped in misery.

The guard took in the scene. I was sure he thought it was more magic. Maybe black magic. He couldn't see that Ree held the door open.

As for magic, I'd been pondering that opportune ember the entire ride home. I was sure there was some kind of magic behind it. But it wasn't mine. I had none. So whose was it? Who else was watching us?

"Catri!" I hastened to the table and put my hands on her shoulders. "Catri, the earl has been kind enough to offer us protection for a few days. This is one of his guards."

Catri looked up at me dully. She still looked the same as when I'd left her. No change in the long hours we'd been gone.

The guard strode to the table and took a closer look at Catri in the candlelight. He had orders to report what he found back to the earl. He'd probably send a messenger back as soon as he went outside.

"How old is she?" He caught Catri's chin and roughly turned her face from side to side, viewing her from all angles.

"Seventeen." I stroked her hair, glad she didn't fight him.

"She looks like she could be your grandma." He sounded disbelieving and there was a vicious scoff in his voice.

I stiffened. "She has the aging illness." I let my tone plead for a little kindness. I brushed the top of her head with a kiss. "Don't worry, Catri. You look much better than you did before the rose."

The soldier dropped his hand from her chin and scrutinized the cottage.

"If you're looking for a flying broomstick, you can relax." I glared at him. "We only have the regular floor sweeping kind here. No potions or toadstools, either."

I hoped he was embarrassed for being so obvious. I stared him down.

He leaned into me. "You should be glad your sister hasn't turned into a beauty."

Was he trying to be kind?

He hustled out the door. It slammed shut behind him.

I was relieved he was gone, but Catri barely seemed to notice. "I need more magic, Mais." Catri looked at me with pleading eyes.

"The rose gave you all it had." I pulled up a chair next to her and took her hands in mine. "We have to count our blessings. You may not be young again, but you're beautiful to me. And for the moment, you're no threat to the earl. Be patient, Cat. The magic may work yet."

Her gaze went to the door. "Are we prisoners in our own home now?"

"Of course not. We're under the earl's protection." I squeezed her hands, but I didn't believe my own words.

"For how long?" She looked tortured.

"Just until the king's party has chosen his next bride. Until the happy party has left. Word is that the king's emissary is almost here. A fortnight from now all will be back to normal."

"So we're not to get a chance at being selectress?"

I was so surprised by her question, and the sound of disappointment in her voice, that I dropped her hands. "No. Does it matter? We have no chance, anyway. We're safer this way. Everyone knows our selectress will be going to her death. It's only a matter of time. She can only hope the king will be merciful in his selection of execution methods."

I didn't mean to sound so harsh, but I was hoping to snap Catri out of the dangerous idea that being our selectress would lead to any kind of happily-ever-after. This king wasn't going to fall in love with his new fiancée, not one of our kind. Our selectress would never be queen.

I wouldn't say Catri was naïve, exactly, but she'd always been too much of a dreamer.

"But our selectress could do so much good." She sounded wistful, but I wasn't believing her altruistic act.

I raised an eyebrow. "True, but?"

"She'll have the best doctors available, the very best. If she ever gets sick..."

"You'd need a different king for that, Cat. Put it out of your mind."

I was bone weary. I got up and went to the upholstered chair in front of the fire. Ree left me alone and let me sit. I should have been hungry, too, but I'd lost all appetite to dreams of sleep.

Ree curled up on a cushion at my feet. "We have much to talk about. I have stories to tell you from my wanderings in the castle."

"Yes, *yes*." But sleep waved before my eyes. The shadows had left the edge of my weariness. Sleep was more enticing than the fear of it was a deterrent.

Ree was suddenly on the alert. He sat up tall. "Look me in the eye."

I was too tired to fight him. I met his eye.

He studied me, then nodded to himself. "The light is coming back to your eyes. Talk can wait. I think it's safe to sleep now..."

I hoped he was right. In any case, I couldn't fight sleep any longer. My head bobbed...

I DIDN'T WAKE until sunrise, and even then, I fought it. Someone had thrown a blanket over me and banked the fire. I was still fully dressed and a little stiff, but I finally felt like I could think again. I'd slept in the chair many nights while Mother was ill and dying. It was surprisingly comfortable.

I looked around, but no Catri. Her bedroom door was closed. She must have covered me and gone to bed.

Ree appeared at my feet, looking as dapper as ever and fully rested. He never seemed to need much sleep. "At last, she wakes. How are you, *sorella*? Get your beauty sleep?"

"As tired as I was, I think that would take a million years or more." I took another quick look around. "It appears we're all still safe and sound."

Ree nodded. "And imprisoned in our own home. Or, you are, anyway. Nothing can stop me from going where I want." He swaggered around the cushion at my feet comically. He tapped his chest. "While you slept, I went out on another intelligence gathering mission. There's much to tell you. It would be best to have our little briefing before your sister wakes."

I rubbed my eyes, but I was perking up. "Yes." He was right, of course. "And I want to hear what you found out at the castle." I yawned and stretched. "I really am eager. If I hadn't been exhausted to death last night..."

Ree waved my apologies aside. "Think nothing of it. A mortal's constitution is weak. The human body can only take so much before it must rest. But I, I need very little. I have a strong constitution."

"Thank goodness," I said, playing to his vanity. "I couldn't say much in the cart on the way home, but you really were brilliant in the earl's office. I would have liked to see him hit in the head with his own reading material, truly I would have." I chuckled at the thought.

Ree looked pleased. "What can I say? Sometimes the mischief of the *munacielli* blends very well with your silly brownie code."

"Let's hope that happens even more often in the future." I stretched again and my stomach growled. It was a good sign that my hunger was returning.

I'd been so tired last night that I hadn't even put my

dagger away or taken my gloves off. Part of me had been afraid to, certainly while the guards could see my hands.

I pulled them off now and studied my hands, half hoping that the magic *had* worn off. But the left hand was just as beautiful as it had been yesterday. Maybe it was more than an illusion. Maybe it was really perfected and permanent. However, my right wrist had a six-fingered bruise across it.

Ree scowled. "You were brave in there, Maisie. The bruises will fade."

I wiggled my fingers and stretched my hands. My left hand moved marvelously well and gracefully. "Look at this, Ree? My left hand moves so well, I might even become lefthanded."

"Not if you know what's good for you." He plopped cross-legged onto the cushion.

Being lefthanded was a sign of consorting with the darkness. It was pure superstition, but you couldn't talk people out of the belief. It would be even worse for me since I'd held the rose with my left hand. People would say I'd soaked up dark magic. Still, the way my hand moved was lovely. It was too bad I didn't have a harp. I bet I could play it with my left hand, even without training. That was how agile my hand felt.

I tucked my hands in my lap. "The earl's castle? What had everyone so upset? Did you manage to find out?"

"Quickly. It was all anyone could talk about. The prince was called back to the palace. He won't be part of the selection party. The earl is naturally disappointed and furious. He spent a great deal of coin thinking he would be entertaining a king, then a prince, and now he'll get nothing more than a high-ranking noble official who he could have entertained on a far smaller budget. And he'll have no chance to bend a prince's ear and win favor with court."

"Is there a problem, then? An emergency in the kingdom?" A prickle of fear shot down my spine.

"From what I gathered, there's no reason to worry. The king is notoriously known for changing his mind and orders. Capricious, they say. And heavily reliant on his brother. Twins and their connection. The king wanted his brother back in the capital for some reason known only to himself.

"The prince was already part way through the Doove before the rider reached him. Word is that he wasn't happy about backtracking."

My thoughts had gone in another direction. That settled it. The young man in the Doove couldn't have been the prince. If the prince had been abducted, it would be all anyone could talk about.

"There was *nothing* about the king's party being attacked by the Fear Dorca? *Nothing* about one of his men gone missing and abducted?" I asked.

"I heard no mention, no gossip of the sort."

I frowned, puzzled.

Ree jumped to his feet. "But there *is* good news. We won't be under house arrest for long. The king's party arrived at the castle late last night. The search for a new selectress begins today."

"Good," I said. "Let's keep that piece of news from Catri for the time being. There's no point in making her more miserable. Even if she's become as beautiful as my hand overnight, she can't be allowed, she won't be allowed, to vie for the king's hand."

I sighed, fearing she'd wake from her sleep a true beauty. Or a monster. Hoping she'd be simply herself as I'd last seen her.

Both beauty and monster were dangerous options right now. Either would lead to her imprisonment and possible death.

Ree read my thoughts. "Should I check in on her?"

Before I could answer, the door to the bedroom swung open. Catri stood in the doorway, except for the expression of utter despair and resignation, looking like she had when I'd dozed off last night. The dark streak in her hair hadn't grown. The rest was still gray. Her face remained as lined.

"You're up." I tried to cover my relief that she was no worse by putting too much sunshine into my voice. "How do you feel this morning? Did you sleep well?"

"The same, Maisie. I slept well, but I feel, and *look*, the same as last night. This is all the magic I'm to expect. I hate that darkling. I *hate* him. If I ever run into him—"

"You'll wisely run in the opposite direction." I forced a smile. Running wouldn't be enough. She'd need a hero, like mine.

While Catri crossed into the kitchen, I whispered to Ree and handed him my dagger. "Return this from where I got it. Then go to town and the castle and be my eyes and ears."

CHAPTER 10
LADY BRINLEY

Lady Brinley Fanger

L I'd always known my father would sacrifice me on the altar of power. It was a daughter's duty to improve the family's situation, no matter the price she would personally pay. I just hadn't thought he'd be so *literal* about it.

Since my twelfth birthday, I'd been betrothed to Arjun Amberflayer, Marquess of Missenlim, the duke's eldest son and heir. My father considered the match quite the coup. I was less enthusiastic. Lord Arjun was neither handsome nor ugly. Nor was he particularly witty nor kind. Or even extremely intelligent. But he was vicious and power hungry like his father, Ermias, which pleased both our fathers, immensely.

Women clamored around Lord Arjun. But as far as I could tell, his main claim to attractiveness was his position and wealth, not his person or personality.

He'd been rumored to be loose with the maids since

puberty first struck him. He consorted with whores. He flirted with ladies and other men's wives. I had no illusions about what marriage to him would be like. My only hope was that after producing several heirs for him, he would leave me alone to pursue my own interests. I would certainly be happy enough for him to pursue his.

In three months, on my eighteenth birthday as proscribed by law, my father and the duke meant to marry us and consolidate the power of both their seats into what would be tantamount to a princedom. And why not? The Royal Circle and the Southern Kingdom would never accept us in their halls of power. We were forever banished behind the Doove, which kept us isolated.

But the Law of Unintended Consequences favored us— while the Doove separated us from the rest of the kingdom, confining us into this harsh climate, we were also protected from attack by the great, dark forest. It was a natural barrier better than any moat or ocean. If we had our own king, which the duke practically was already, what could The Royal Circle do? And why should they bother? The tax money we sent to the palace was a pittance compared to other provinces, a mere drop in the royal treasury.

Though if the palace knew the plans my father and the duke had for alliances with other kingdoms and the trade they would establish...

Neither my father nor the duke trusted the other, but the sheer magnitude of the power the combination of their territories would create forced them into the marriage contract. A betrothal was legally binding, only a king could break it. But it also wasn't a marriage.

I was pure and untouched. Just what a king like King Kylan IV would want in a bride. And he was, by law, free to choose me as his next selectress if he so wished.

The king's edict commanded that all single young ladies between the ages of sixteen and twenty-two in the province, betrothed or not, present themselves as candidates for selectress and his hand. He wanted the choicest of us all and the largest choice available to him.

Even so, we were sparsely populated. The farther north one went, the sparser the population grew. Only the duke's territory had more people than ours. The king's choice from the southern lands and territories of our village were limited, at best. Fewer than fifty young women from father's territory, perhaps three times that many from the duke's. The rest of the province was hardly worth traversing unless the king was very desperate not to take a wife any time soon.

From the moment the edict arrived on the wings of the sad news of the latest selectress's death, everyone in The Outlands knew I would be chosen next. We were first on the route north out of the Doove, but there wouldn't be any need for his men to go farther.

No one even bothered to doubt that I would be the king's choice. I'd been raised to be a duchess, the most powerful woman of the region. Without meaning to brag, simply stating the truth with all due modesty, my accomplishments were many. I could sing and dance and play all manner of musical instruments. My embroidery was as fine as anyone's north of the Doove. I'd been taught to smile and flatter and charm men while not appearing too forward or ever crossing the line into impropriety or impurity.

I could read and do sums. I'd been trained to manage a large estate. I'd been schooled in manners and the ways of court, such as we understood them. I had the finest clothes available here and was always beautifully turned out.

But most important of all, I'd been bred for beauty. And the king wanted a beautiful wife.

What a fool to prize that above all else, especially when I, and so many young ladies of my acquaintance, had so much more to offer—love and loyalty. Intelligence and good sense. Even large dowries if one was inclined to be mercenary about things. Which seemed more of an incentive to marry than fleeting beauty.

My father had married far below his station in pursuit of the goal of turning out handsome sons and beautiful daughters, trying to breed out the valor of his ancestors that had produced the six-fingered curse. My poor ancestors were probably rolling in their graves at the knowledge that the current earl was ashamed of their sacrifices.

Father had succeeded only in producing one living child—me. He had five stillborn sons and three more stillborn girls. Breeding for beauty wasn't as easy as it seemed. The curse ran strong and killed the weaker stock. I was now his only hope.

Father had been in a foul mood ever since word had come that the king's party was coming *through* the Doove, not *around* it. If the Doove could be breached, or traversed in this case, so easily, the plans Father had made with the duke were in peril. We weren't as isolated as we'd imagined. Further, what did safe passage mean? Only one possible thing—a treaty with the Fairy Queen. That was a danger no one wanted to imagine.

I twisted my hands in my lap as I waited for Mariah, my lady's maid, to bring me breakfast and dress me and do my hair. I studied my hands—so close to having only five fingers each. The sixth was barely noticeable. But barely noticeable wasn't good enough.

I'd never dreamed, none of us had, that anyone from my generation here in The Outlands would have a chance of being a selectress or queen. Yes, we had a young, eligible king. But there were too many other provinces in the line of succession ahead of us for any of us to have serious queenly dreams. Girls ten years younger than me had a chance in the future, maybe, if a queen died in childbed. Those just being born had an even better chance to wed a prince in the future. Or so we had all thought.

Then the king's first selectress drowned in a crystal-clear bathing pool in the king's private lagoon. She'd been found with her long hair floating around her, looking peaceful and beautiful to the end. No one could imagine how the accident had happened. From all accounts, she was an accomplished swimmer. There was no sign of a struggle or violence. Even the court physicians mystified.

The next selectress fell down a flight of stone stairs to her death. She made a beautifully tragic picture, we heard, lying at the bottom of the stairs with her golden hair and skirts fanned around her.

The third choked on a bone in front of king and court at a banquet in her honor. Unlike the other two, not a pretty death at all. But then, she'd been the least pretty of all of them to begin with. Hers weren't a handsome people. Why should anyone have believed the king would wed and bed *her*?

That left us next up, between the king and the woman he was rumored to love. Some of our people were beautiful, in the king's standard, but none of us were perfect. And the new queen had to be *both*.

I thought our people were *all* beautiful, each in their own way, beautiful *and* each unique. To top it off, we had beautiful spirits as well. We were known for our charity and kindness, for seeing past appearances. At least we had been, until the ways of the court began invading our culture and permeating our corporate thinking.

I loved the variety in our people and would have done anything to preserve it—the gentle wave of a too-short arm, the gleam in the single eye of an old man, an extra finger or toe here and there. What other province could boast of such a range of looks and talents?

After the third selectress died, Father and the duke had talked of at least bedding Lord Arjun and me quickly to secure their power. There was no need to take a chance of me being chosen. The king could be angered, but he was far away on the other side of the Doove. By the time he, or his team, reached us, any initial anger would have cooled. The king would certainly understand the passions of the young. Then word came that the king's party was coming through the Doove, and it became apparent that we *could* suffer the king's wrath. Further, that his emissary would be here sooner than anticipated. Any perturbance to my chastity now would look planned and be a blatant insult to His Majesty.

Father realized something else. Unlike the duke, he had another shot at power, *more* power. The other families of dead selectresses had all been heavily compensated and given a voice at court. Father had no other heirs and Mother refused to die so he could marry again to obtain some. What did Father expect to get upon my death? My mother's death, too? A pretty, young wife and a nursery full of heirs to replace me?

As for me, I could only hope my death would be pretty and painless. That I would look like a princess while I lay in state and was then carried to be buried in the royal tomb.

I looked down at my hands again. No matter how beautiful I was, the king wouldn't take a chance of me producing a "deformed" heir.

The scent of rose filled the air, carried on a whiff of smoke. Of course, it was past rose season. Father was burning the Doove Rose. The whole castle was perfumed with the scent.

The outcast girl, Maisie, had brought it to him. I'd seen her in the great room while she waited for her audience with Father. We'd played together as children. For a brief time. Until Father found out about it. Then Mother had taught me it was better, safer, for Maisie and her family as well as for us, if I ignored her. If I forgot I'd ever known her. She probably thought I was arrogant when I passed her by, unacknowledged. But really, I'd been protecting her.

Since her arrival, and since she'd turned over the rose,

I'd been careful not to eat or drink anything that Mariah hadn't carefully screened for me. Yes, I'd heard the rumors that Maurelle had pronounced the rose poisoned with dark magic.

I didn't think Father would be desperate enough to try the rose magic on me to rid me of my little stubs of extra fingers, not when it was now rumored to be contaminated by a darkling. He could have ruined me and made a real monster of me. Even damaged as I was, I was too valuable an asset to risk. But I took no chances.

Father had sent plenty of his men after the rose. Fearless, well-trained soldiers and guards. They'd fended off the rest of the villagers but had come home emptyhanded. How had Maisie defeated them?

Father had been furious. He'd been intent on making me even more beautiful, with two five-fingered hands and no curse. As an added benefit, he meant to prevent any other young woman from using the rose to her benefit.

Then Maisie had dumped the rose right into his lap and all it had cost him was a gold coin and a tiny bottle of his prize whisky. Nothing at all, really.

First thing this morning, he'd sent proclamations to the village to be posted conspicuously and abundantly. They stated that the reward had been claimed and the rose was being destroyed because it had been poisoned by the touch of a darkling. Even now, the scent of the burning would perfume the village, as well as be proof of rose's destruction.

Mariah told me as she was dressing me for bed last night that the witch Maurelle had paid Father a visit after Maisie left, warning him to bury it. And offering to take it off his hands. Father had been wily enough not to trust her. He had consulted with his own magician, who recommended burning it at sunrise. We could only hope Father's magician was correct.

The was a light tap on the door. Mariah entered with my breakfast tray. She closed the door with her hip and set the tray in front of me. "The king's entourage arrived late last night, my lady. Their carriage and horses are in the stable, along with a contingency of soldiers. Lord Noblett is your father's guest. He was expecting to see you at breakfast, but your father won us some time, pleading the unexpected early arrival, so that you can beautify yourself. Everyone understands the importance of the first impression you make on him."

"Thank you, Mariah." So that was what caused the commotion that woke me in the middle of the night. I had hoped there was another explanation. "How do they look, these men who braved the Doove? Are they monsters now?"

"*Hardly*, my lady." She blushed, which meant at least one of the men had already been flirting with her, trying to pry information about me from her.

"Why did they arrive so late?" I asked, more to myself than her. "It's horribly rude. Were they chased out of the Doove by the monsters therein?"

"They made their excuses, saying only that the king is eager for his new fiancée, so all haste had to be made to get here."

I looked at her sharply.

Her blush deepened. "They appear in good spirits,

laughing and joking. None of them seem the least frightened by their journey through the woods."

That meant nothing good. It was practically an admission that the Fairy Queen had protected them.

"They look perfectly fine, *very* fine, if you will," Mariah said on a wistful breath. "Beautiful, each of them. They have the scullery and lower maids atwitter."

I bet they did.

"All the maids and staff have been warned to stay away from them."

Good for our housekeeper for watching out for our staff.

"The new arrivals all think highly of themselves." Mariah wrinkled her nose, showing her good sense despite her apparent immediate infatuation with them. "A tumble with one of our kind is likely beneath them."

"A tumble is almost always beneath the man," I said, dryly.

Mariah didn't bother blushing or admonishing me. "Your father wants you primed and looking gorgeous. The maroon silk, I think."

I nodded. "Father hopes Lord Noblett will take one look at me and make his decision immediately, not even bothering to look further."

"He's under no obligation to look farther," Mariah said. "I overheard him telling the earl. The king apparently gave Lord Noblett complete power to make the selection at his discretion. Your father looked pleased."

"Father would send me to my marriage bed so easily." We both knew I meant he'd send me to my death.

The very real thought of throwing this interview had

crossed my mind more than once. Make myself as ugly as possible. Laugh like a hyena. Make stupid comments. Come down dressed hideously. But Father would kill me then, or worse. And whatever punishment he meted out wouldn't be pretty in any way. Death might even be preferable.

Mariah picked up my hairbrush.

I picked up my fork. "Let the condemned eat their last meal in freedom."

I fought to appear calm, but my mind was furiously trying to think of a way to escape my fate.

CHAPTER 11
LORD NOBLETT'S VISIT

Lady Brinley

L I made Lord Noblett wait to meet me, stretching out my stay of execution as long as possible. Once I was selected, how long until they whisked me away? How many more days did I have on this earth until I was found beautifully posed, but very dead?

Outside my window in the courtyard below, the men from the Royal Circle exercised their horses and polished the elaborate carriage they'd brought. Had it housed the prince until he was called back to the palace?

The prince, too, was rumored to be the most handsome man in the kingdom, maybe even more so than his brother the king. Of course, to say so was practically treason so it was only whispered about in a joking tone. Plausible deniability for all.

Frankly, I was disappointed that I hadn't gotten to see for myself. Though I would get my chance soon enough.

And I had better prefer the king, for all the good that would do me.

It was hard to imagine men more handsome, or more handsomely turned out, than those in the courtyard below. Both men and horses were the most gorgeous specimens I'd ever seen. Man and animal were muscle and sinew, grace and speed, dark manes, and high spirits.

My heart lurched at the sight of them, and my pulse quickened. I scolded myself for being so shallow, for having my head turned by a handsome face, many handsome faces.

The carriage, too, was something to behold—trimmed with gold and studded with jewels, embossed with the king's crest and seal, and made for speed and comfort. Rumor had it, too, that this was only one of the king's lesser coaches. He wouldn't risk his best on a mission like this, but a state carriage was necessary for this mission and appearances.

If everything in the court was this fine, it was hard to imagine how handsome the king was, or how I would ever fit in. Even as an earl's daughter, I felt shabby.

It was rumored that the first selectress had gone blindly to the king, unprepared for anything but for him to do his duty and marry her. The second selectress had gone to the Royal Circle prepared with the most potent love potion any of her sorcerers could brew.

But it had been for naught. The king seemed immune. Most likely, his own wizards had cast protection spells around him.

The third selectress had taken a lesson from both and

had had herself encased in a charm spell. That hadn't worked, either.

I was to have gone enchanted by the Doove Rose to be an irresistible beauty, gorgeous in any man's eyes no matter his tastes. Only as a backup I had a passion potion that Father's man had made for me, a potion made to make the king lust for me whether I was beautiful or not.

The thought was that a love potion had been too bold, emotions too hard to manipulate, and charm was too weak. But lust was another matter, primal and fleshly. Lust didn't require a thought process. It merely wanted and took.

I asked for some affection to be added to the potion. If I could tempt the king to my bed before marriage *and* win his affection, he might simply put me aside as a mistress and take some other girl from the province as selectress to kill without wedding. As mistress, I could have perhaps even *more* influence than as queen and wife. Even Father saw the brilliance of the plan.

Success was a faint hope, but it was the best I had now that the rose had been ruined.

All of our human magic was weak. What I really needed was fairy magic, but that wasn't even in the realm of possibility. I would have to make do with brewed herbs, aphrodisiacs, and incantations.

My father sent Larkus, the butler, for me. I jumped when he tapped on my door. "The earl wishes you to join him and Lord Noblett in the library, my lady. Immediately."

There was no use protesting that I needed more time. Larkus could clearly see that Mariah was idling time away, mindlessly straightening my room, and I was dressed and coiffed. That my jewels sparkled at my neck and ears and in my hair.

I nodded, rose, and followed him out, leaving Mariah behind with an anguished, yet hopeful, look.

The library was a comfortable room with a roaring fire and walls completely covered by shelves and shelves of books that very few of us in the household read. Father had never been a big reader and Mother had long since given up. All the volumes were leatherbound with gold gilt embossing. I felt a shadow of guilt that I hadn't taken the opportunity to learn something from them. Something that might help me now.

Lord Noblett sat in front of the fire with his back toward the door, talking with Father. When I entered, he rose and turned to face me. He must have been nearly as old as Father, but Lord Noblett looked much younger. He was a handsome man by any standard and more finely dressed than any of us, with ruffles at his neck and cuffs and fine gold thread woven through his coat and breeches.

He had the look of the Royal Circle about him—everything perfect, straight nose, straight, white teeth, perfectly trimmed beard, perfectly set eyes, everything in pleasing proportion. While beautiful and perfect, he didn't look quite natural. So it was with the nobles and people of the Royal Circle. They looked almost manufactured. Too finely carved to be real.

"There she is," Father said. "Lord Noblett, my daughter, Brinley."

My skirts whispered as I walked across the carpet and

bowed before Lord Noblett. When I rose, he tipped my chin to get a good look at my face.

Our eyes met. He studied me with a placid expression, but I didn't see pleasure in his eyes, only disappointment.

"Very lovely," he whispered in a voice that was just as beautiful as the rest of him, deep and silky with the cultured accent of the Royal Circle. "It's a pleasure." He took both my hands in his and raised them to his lips.

It was a gesture of gallantry, but I couldn't help but feel that it was also an opportunity to get a good, close look at my "deformity," my lovely beauty mark.

He held my hands a little longer than necessary, rubbing his thumbs gently over them. Finally, he released them. "I'm pleased you'll be joining us for the selecting today, Lady Brinley. I've sent a team ahead to the village to assemble the eligible young women." Lord Noblett smiled, but it didn't reach his eyes. "You, of course, must ride in the carriage with me." He held his hand out for me.

My father's jaw ticked. He was furious.

My heart stopped. This wasn't supposed to happen. I was supposed to be anointed here and *now*.

Lord Noblett seemed fully aware of our shock and discomfort and seemed to be enjoying it. "Just a formality," he said, smoothly. "We can't select a queen without giving *every* young lady the appearance of her chance. Not when so many of them have travelled so far. Good relations with the people. The king is all about good relations. We don't want to invite a rebellion, do we?" He laughed like he'd just told a good joke, but his gaze slid to my father.

A shiver ran down my spine. We were in even more

danger than I'd thought. Word of Father's rebellious plans had reached the palace.

THE VILLAGE of Norwallsend was named for its location at the northern end of Bede's Wall, a stone wall defensive fortification built by the ancient southern ruler, Emperor Tartus, before the kingdom was united. Bede's Wall was supposed to keep the fae in their realm. But, of course, it never had. Now Bede's Wall disappeared deep into the Doove, which had overtaken it centuries ago. The wall had been one more fortification that my father had been counting on to protect us when he and the duke started our own kingdom. But it had proven as unreliable as the Doove now, too.

Our people being banned north of Bede's Wall had been just one more aspect of our punishment. The kingdom had never extended north of the wall into the wild before we'd been settled here. But here we were now, established and thriving in our own way on the barren land and in the cold climate, much to the rest of the kingdom's dismay.

I sat in the carriage on a velvet seat next to Lord Noblett. In his lap sat a huge black leather ledger that seemed to be making my father, who sat stiffly across from us, nervous. Accounts settled? What did my father owe? Was this a tax collection excursion as well? A time to collect overdue tributes to His Majesty?

Father and I were both wondering, or at least I was, and I assumed he was, whether we were being punished for his plans of rebellion. Was Lord Noblett just toying with us to put Father in his place? Or were we to be truly punished?

Lord Noblett and his men looked just as merry and unfazed as Mariah had described. The trip through the Doove had done them no apparent harm. It may have even done them good. They now had bragging rights, and stories of bravery, to build into legends. I heard one soldier bragging about the enormous bear he had killed single-handedly. But I wondered, was that magic, too? Had the Fairy Queen erased the terrors of the trip from their minds and replaced them with memories of valor?

As we approached, it was apparent that Norwallsend was lit for a festival. The fall day was cloudy and cool and threatening rain, but that only made the autumn leaves stand out brighter and more colorful against the dull sky.

The young women vying for the king's hand were already lined up along the town square. The gray skies made their colorful dresses look that much more festive and flattered their figures that much more. Scarves and skirts fluttered like delicate fall leaves.

A fire was lit in the great stone fireplace in the center of the town square. Norwallsend smelled of roasting pig and chestnuts, and spicy festival cakes baking in the community ovens, with just a hint of the rose perfume still clinging in the air. Children ran around in front of the young women, waving long ribbons along the procession route. Young men jogged alongside our carriage in a kind of competition to see who could keep up with us the longest.

I waved from the carriage window, smiling a smile I

didn't feel and observing my competition with a critical, but sympathetic eye.

It was my duty to beat these women out for the king's hand. But it was also my duty to protect them. In this case, the goals aligned nicely. A poor girl had no hope of a lust potion of her own. I, at least, had that.

I knew all the young women from the Norwallsend area at least by sight. Those from farther afield were unfamiliar to me.

A group of Lord Noblett's men had come ahead to organize the production. They'd lined the young women up according to their own standard of beauty from plainest at the end of the line on the fringes of the square to prettiest nearest the center by the stage. Class made little difference.

The mood in the village was full of false gaiety and false pride at the supposed honor of our term of succession. Though all the young women had gone to great lengths to look as pretty as possible, their mothers and fathers hugged them close. They watched the carriage approach with smiles, but their eyes sparkled with fear and hatred.

Fashion ran the gamut from the folksy homespun of the poorest to my finery as the daughter of an earl. Most did their best to hide their beauty marks, but a few...

Lord Noblett's face clouded as he spotted a girl who had emphasized her third arm by encasing it in a bright sleeve and a stack of bracelets. She was playing a lute with two hands and waving and blowing kisses with the third. She blew one directly at the carriage and Lord Noblett.

I fought a wave of fear. *Rebellion. Open rebellion.*

I caught Lord Noblett's arm, trying to distract him. "I've never seen such a welcome from the people of Norwallsend. You'll have to relay to His Majesty how much he's loved here."

It was false. And Lord Noblett knew it. But we all had to keep up the pretenses. It worked to distract him from the young woman. *For the moment.* I hope she showed more sense when he did his inspection.

The carriage came to a halt in the center of the square at the end of the line of women. A footman opened the door. Lord Noblett handed me out. I caught my full skirts as the footman helped me down. Lord Noblett came out behind me, followed by his page, and escorted me to the front of the line, where I took my place as the most beautiful.

I relaxed. Lord Noblett had now clearly only been toying with us. How could he choose any other than the woman at the end of the line of beauty? Anything else would only be an insult to His Majesty.

A small stage and podium had been setup. My father made a welcoming speech and introduced Lord Noblett. Lord Noblett gave a speech of his own, introducing the procedure for choosing our selectress. His page stood next to him with a velvet cushion displaying the ring the king had sent for the chosen selectress. Even beneath the gray skies, it dazzled and drew the eye.

Lord Noblett seemed oblivious to the way the ring took the people's attention off him. He was obviously comfortable in his roll, but his charm was oily and too polished. The best that could be said was that he was a typical politician.

When his speech was finished, he alighted from the stage, and walked to the end of the line with his page and another servant in tow. The page carried the ring. The other servant carried the official ledger.

Lord Noblett paused in front of each young woman and asked her name. The page then made a checkmark in the ledger. Lord Noblett asked a few questions and made a little small talk while the servant stood by quietly showing off the ring. Lord Noblett paid innocuous compliments. He paused longer with each young woman as he made his way up the line toward me. When he finished questioning the candidate, he took her left hand, and kissed it lightly, ever the courtier. Then he thanked her for coming out today and relayed the king's gratitude and appreciation.

Even with all of that, the process went amazingly quickly. As he made his way toward me, my heart tried to beat its way out of my chest. Despite my racing heart, I kept my chin high, and my expression poised and relaxed.

As Lord Noblett moved to a new girl, the last one nearly always visibly relaxed, but looked longingly after the ring. Its beauty drew the eye as if enchanted. That value of that ring was more than the value of the entire worth of the village. Even so, each young woman's loved ones squeezed her shoulders, relieved. The danger was past.

My father stood rigidly by me. He hadn't allowed my mother to come. She was left at the castle to supervise the engagement banquet that would be held in my honor after.

Finally, Lord Noblett came to me. "I already know this beauty." He took my left hand and kissed it.

His page made a check in the ledger.

I waited for the pronouncement. I waited for him to put that dazzling ring of power on my finger. To signify me as the most important woman in the kingdom.

A dark look crossed Lord Noblett's face. He stepped aside and whispered something to his page, who answered in hushed tones.

Lord Noblett's expression became even darker. He broke away from his page and faced my father. "This isn't everyone. Where are Maisie Jayne Rose and Catri Weaver?"

CHAPTER 12

THE SELECTRESS IS CHOSEN

M*aisie*

Ree appeared out of breath and out of nowhere, crashing into the table clumsily where I sat peeling potatoes for stew. His lack of composure was completely unlike him. I'd never seen him flustered like this before.

His face was flushed. His coat was askew and his hair windblown. He looked as if he'd run a very long way. Like all the way from Norwallsend.

Ree, running over cobblestones? *Unthinkable.*

"*Hurry. Hide.* They're coming for you." Ree glanced at Catri by the fire. "*Both* of you."

"*Who?*" But I knew. Of course, I knew. With a fear that made my throat go dry and my heart momentarily stop. Today was the selection day and Catri and I had skipped it. At the earl's command. We couldn't have gotten past our "protectors" even if we'd wanted to, but I'd given my word that we wouldn't.

"Who do you think? Lord Noblett, the king's emissary." Ree flit around, bolting the door. "I've just come from the selecting. Everyone expected Lord Noblett to come to town and pronounce Lady Brinley the selectress. The selection was just a formality, probably to test loyalties. But he insisted on inspecting all the candidates. We thought for show. To make it appear that every young woman had a fair chance.

"He lined all the young women up and walked the line, going through everyone, even Lady Brinley, and made no selection. He wants to see you and Catri. He looked furious that you weren't there."

I swallowed hard against the lump of fear in my throat. I glanced at Catri. "I promised the earl that neither of us would present ourselves as candidates for the king's hand. I thought he would have explained to Lord Noblett, made some excuse why we're ineligible or unsuitable."

I was desperately trying to grasp what this turn of events meant. There was no one more beautiful, or from a more powerful family, than Lady Brinley. She was the superior candidate. No one denied it.

I had to be brave for Catri. I tried to seem unconcerned. "What if Lord Noblett insists on seeing us?" I shrugged. "I don't see the danger. The earl can rest easy. The rose has failed us. Neither of us are competition for Lady Brinley."

Catri rose from her chair. She lifted her chin. "I'm going to fix up and present myself with dignity. If the king wants an older woman, I'm his girl. Who am I to deny him his choice of all of us?"

She'd been in a sullen mood since realizing she was as

young looking as she was going to get. That she was stuck as a late middle-aged woman.

"No, Catri. You can't."

She ignored me and headed to the bedroom to change.

I swore beneath my breath. What were Lord Noblett and the king up to? And the earl? Did he now mean to sacrifice one of us to the king? Surely no one would care that an "old woman" like Catri died before her time. But what of the earl's quest for power and influence?

On the other side, was Lord Noblett intent on making fools of us all by selecting Catri for the king to scorn openly? Was this some kind of new strategy for breaking the line of selection? And us, the entire province? Was the king aching for a reason to bring his wrath down on us?

See what I have to put up with as candidates for queen? It's time to end this madness. Time to end the line of selection.

I tried to go after Catri. Ree blocked my path. "Let her go. Protect yourself."

I stared at him. "I'm in no danger of being selected."

"There's no guarantee of that, not in this crazy world. Lord Noblett is up to something." Ree's voice was low and flat. Ominous.

I couldn't argue with him.

"Lord Noblett is looking for something. He kissed the left hand of every young lady who presented herself." Ree lifted an eyebrow. "He'll want to see yours."

I went cold. "Maybe it's just coincidence."

"*Maybe*. Kissing the left hand *is* a tradition in the Royal Circle. Even so, you can't let him in the house." Ree held his ground. "You can't present yourself. You can't let him choose you. And you must protect yourself for the case that Lord Noblett doesn't select you. You can't give the earl any reason to have your head instead."

Ree tapped his chin. "We'll have to make an excuse, something that disqualifies you. Something that will make Lord Noblett take Lady Brinley. Something that Lord Fanger will verify."

My mind raced, but I couldn't think of anything.

Ree paced.

The sound of a horse neighing outside made me jump. Hooves thundered on the road in front of the croft, mixed with the sound of carriage wheels bumping over uneven road. The thump of boots on our porch. The sound of male voices, pulling up horses and shouting commands.

"Giant hogweed." Ree's gaze was focused out the back window on our small field.

"Hogweed?" I pondered the suggestion. "*Yes.*" I spoke mostly to myself. As I weighed the wisdom of Ree's suggestion, a sense of calm settled over me.

"In the garden." Ree nodded. "You got into it in the garden or the field yesterday. You must stay out of the sun for a week or more or your skin will burn and scar. You can blame it on me, your terrible *munacielli*, a real trickster. Terrible. I put it there for you to stumble into unaware."

The soft spot in my heart for him grew. "You're a genius, Ree Ree." Even as I spoke, I frowned. "But will they look for it?"

"Don't worry. I can take care of that." He grabbed a blanket and tossed it to me. "Cover yourself from head to toe. Even your face. Don't give them any reason to suspect a lie."

I began wrapping the blanket around myself. "*Catri.* Will *she* back me up?"

"I have superior powers of suggestion. I'll convince her. They're about to knock. Hold your ground." Ree bounded off toward Catri's bedroom just as a loud rap shook the front door.

I pulled a doily that Mother had crotched from our one small end table and tossed over my head and face as a veil. I steeled myself. "Who's there?" As if I didn't know and fear.

"Open up by order of King Kylan IV and Lord Fanger, the earl of the realm." The voice was steady, fierce, official, and male.

As I hesitated, Catri strolled from her room, dressed in all her finery, her hair up and done. I couldn't believe she'd gotten ready so quickly. I suspected Ree had something to do with it.

She brushed past me and flung the door wide open.

A nobleman and his page stood on our stoop, flanked by soldiers in the king's livery. The earl's men had stepped down and back.

The page spoke. "Lord Noblett is here to interview Catri Weaver and Maisie Jayne Rose for the position of selectress. Are your daughters at home, ma'am?"

"Daughters?" Catri lifted her chin proudly. "I'm an unmarried maid. *I'm* Catri Weaver."

I huddled in the shadows of the corner, watching in horror.

Lord Noblett's eyes narrowed.

The earl appeared on the stoop behind him. As he caught a glimpse of Catri, he seemed to relax ever so slightly. "She is who she says, my lord. She has the aging disease, but she is yet young."

Lord Noblett scowled.

"Traveling is difficult for a woman of her apparent age. Which is why, as I explained, I didn't call her to the village," the earl said in a supercilious tone.

I had to hand it to the earl, he had guts to speak to Lord Noblett like that. And he thought on his feet.

Lord Noblett held out his hand. "Your left hand, ma'am."

Catri held hers out with a smile, letting Lord Noblett take it and lift it to his lips.

"A kiss from the king. My apologies for disturbing you." He glanced around the room and spotted me skulking in the shadows. "Maisie Jayne Rose?"

Catri turned over her shoulder to look at me. "That's she. My sister. You must forgive her. She can't come into the light. She accidentally got into a patch of giant hogweed yesterday while bringing the cow in from the field. The burrs and sap got all over her before she noticed. She's lucky none got in her eyes, or she'd be blind. We got her washed up with soap and water immediately. No burns, fortunately. But now the light will burn her delicate skin. She has to stay out of the sun for at least a week or more."

Catri looked surprised by the words that had come out of her mouth, as if she hadn't meant to speak them at all.

Good job, Ree!

I nodded miserably. "I've no idea where the hogweed came from. Blew out of the Doove, I imagine. It's always throwing weeds our way unexpectedly. I'm sorry, my lord, but I couldn't present myself in this condition."

Lord Noblett brushed past Catri into the croft, striding to where I shrunk into the corner. "You didn't mention this, Fanger."

The earl followed him in. "Hogweed's a problem in the province, my lord. Get into a patch and it can scar and blind as they say. Very nasty weed."

Lord Noblett studied me in my shapeless wrappings with my hands gloved and tucked neatly away in the folds, and my doily veil covering my face. His eyes were very narrow. He held out his hand. "Your left hand."

I held out my gloved hand.

"Take the glove off."

I shook my head. "I'm sorry, my lord. But I can't expose you to it, nor can I bare it to the light. Not for a week or more until the danger of burning has passed."

He crossed his arms. "I can wait. I must see something of your skin. It's the law."

I didn't want him lingering in the province for a week or more. I certainly didn't want him standing in my home with his arms crossed for an instant more than he had to. I couldn't afford to let him wait until I was "healed" from the toxins of the hogweed.

I bit my lip. "Would a finger do? My baby finger is the only part of my hand unaffected."

"A finger will suffice." He waved his hand, signaling me to hurry.

I defiantly pulled the glove off my baby finger. What harm could the sight of so small a finger do, especially in the dim light of the corner? Give him what he wants and let him go. Who in their right mind would choose the king's wife, judge her the most beautiful woman in the province, based on the tip of a little finger, even a beautiful little finger?

I held it out for him, arrogantly, like a posh woman of stature.

He lifted my mostly gloved hand to his face and kissed my finger with a tickling brush of his moustache. He held my gloved hand, staring at my finger uncomfortably long. A grin creased his face, lighting his eyes, and lifting the corners of his moustache. He looked almost bewitched.

His gaze rose from the tip of my finger to my veiled eyes. "Congratulations, Miss Rose. You're going to be our next queen."

My blood ran cold. I went into shock and stumbled back against the wall.

Behind him, the earl paled with anger. I thought he might draw his sword and slay me right there. Catri let out a canting cry of anguish.

I pulled my hand back. "*No.* I don't want to be queen. I'm not beautiful. I'm not born and bred to be queen. My sister needs me here, as you can see."

"Your little finger says otherwise," Lord Noblett said.

I reached to unwrap my blanket. Ree appeared, stepping into the room from thin air, pulling at my skirts for me to stop.

"When you're settled in the palace, you can send for your sister. She'll have the best physicians and magicians to attend to her. In the meantime, the earl will look after her." He turned over his shoulder to the earl. "Won't you, Lord Fanger?"

The earl nodded, but his jaw was ticking. He was furious. If Lord Noblett's men hadn't been with him, I was sure the earl would have tried to kill him, king's man or no.

I froze. Did I believe him? Could I trust him? Was it possible to help Catri before I died in some mysterious way?

The look on Lord Noblett's face was pure evil delight. He was issuing me a challenge to discard my blanket and drop the charade. If I did, I had no doubt that he'd order his men to stab me through in front of my sister and the earl. It was a capital crime to lie to the king's agent.

I pulled my blanket tighter around me and lowered my face to cover my anger and fear.

Lord Noblett laughed softly. "Good. That's better. What do you think now of being chosen selectress?"

"I'm honored, my lord." I choked the words out.

"That's more like it. The king will appreciate how humble you are. Humility is a valuable trait in a wife, especially the wife of so great a king." He pulled a velvet ring box from his pocket and opened it to reveal a betrothal ring of purest gold sitting in a bed of black velvet.

It was the most beautiful ring, the most beautiful *thing*, I'd ever seen. It was so brilliant and stunning that I swore it actually spoke to me audibly. Surely it was whispering my name. *Queen Maisie. Queen Maisie...*

I glanced at Catri. She was dazzled by the ring, but she didn't appear to hear anything.

I took a step back with a hand to my throat. The ring had a terrible beauty—dark and seductive, a mirror of the soul. A center diamond caught the light tantalizingly. It was surrounded by deep green emeralds, rubies the color of blood, and dark blue sapphires like the clear night sky.

Lord Noblett motioned impatiently for me to give him my hand.

"But I'm gloved," I protested, with my left hand still pressed against the hollow of my throat. "It won't fit—"

He took a step into me and wrenched my hand free roughly. He felt up my fingers through my gloves. "Such small, slight fingers. The ring is sized large to accommodate any hand. It will fit." With a swift motion, he jammed it onto my ring finger over my glove. "As the king's agent, with the power vested in me by His Majesty as his trusted servant, I pronounce you selectress of the realm and betrothed of His Majesty, King Kylan IV."

I gasped and stared at the ring, temporarily mesmerized, as the bizarre pronouncement rang in my ears.

"The ring will size itself in time." He motioned for his guards as he held fast to my elbow. "Escort our next queen to the carriage. We leave for The Royal Circle immediately."

"*No.*" I shook my head. "I need time to pack. I need time to get my household in order. To make sure Catri has everything she needs—"

He shoved me at the guards. "There's nothing of your shabby belongings and clothing fit to wear before the king. Fortunately, His Majesty is a generous, thoughtful man. As a token of his affection, the king has sent a chest of gowns, made by the king's own trusted tailor, for his chosen bride. We have a seamstress in our party who can make any necessary adjustments. You need bring nothing. All will be provided."

I reached out for Catri, but one of the guards stepped forward and grabbed me. He tossed me over his shoulder and headed toward the door.

"Catri!" I stretched out to her with tears in my eyes.

Catri's eyes locked onto the ring on my hand. She wouldn't meet my eye.

Ree ran after us. "I'll take care of her, *sorella*. You take care of yourself."

"No. *No!*" I kicked and screamed, but the guard stuffed me into the waiting carriage and locked me in with the click of a golden handle.

Lord Noblett mounted his waiting horse and nodded to the driver of the carriage. The driver clucked to the horses. The carriage jolted forward.

I held my wrappings tightly and tucked my ringed hand into my blanket out of sight, wishing I at least had the protection of Mother's dagger. But I was defenseless.

I looked out the window, hoping for a final glimpse of Catri. But she was nowhere to be seen. She hadn't come out to see me carted off.

I slunk into the corner of the seat in the shadows like a woman truly afraid of the light. I was almost too stunned and shocked for rational thought. How had my baby finger enchanted Lord Noblett against my will? Was the Doove Rose full of dark magic even *before* the Fear Dorca touched it?

And most worrying of all—what was I going to do when Lord Noblett discovered that I was *not* beautiful?

The Saga Continues...

NEXT UP: A narrow escape. A flight out of darkness. Into the light and a realm beyond imagination and wonder. But is the Seelie Realm prepared for *The Grayling Fae*?

Get THE GRAYLING FAE!

Made in United States
North Haven, CT
18 July 2022

21522533R00087